From the Fires
Scattered There

A Novel

Kammeron Polverari

ISBN: 978-1-957723-94-5 (hard cover)
        978-1-957723-95-2 (soft cover)

Edited by: Karli Jackson

Published by Warren Publishing
Charlotte, NC
www.warrenpublishing.net
Printed in the United States

For Truett

Chapter One

The silver-and-purple East Coast Champion slid into the Charleston, South Carolina, train depot with its brakes shrill and shrieking and the rails quivering under its weight. The gray sky hung low with clouds and memories, laden with anticipation of what was waiting, or not waiting, at the other end of the tracks.

He should just step out in front of the train, he told himself. Then it wouldn't matter what was or was not at the end of the tracks. Just one quick step, and even at this waning speed, the front of the train could easily toss him up and throw him back down on the tracks and roll over him and maul him and sever him into pieces. It would be a slow reckoning, and he deserved every morsel of it. He looked around to see if anyone was watching. Just a couple of long strides, a quick leap, and then it would be done. Over.

No, he chided himself, *we've already discussed this. You have to try again. You owe them that, at least. Try again. If it doesn't happen, if it doesn't work out, then let the train pulverize you into pieces. You're nothing but pieces now anyway.*

So instead of terminating his life, James Merritt tightened his grip on the olive-green rucksack and repositioned the canvas strap over his shoulder. The train was three minutes late when it finally hissed into the station, steam billowing from its belly in quick, fuming puffs, a steed racing into its stall. James checked his Pullman ticket against the painted number eight on the side of the train and took an impatient step toward it before it crept to a complete stop. *It would have been so simple*, he thought.

The December wind picked up his coat collar and held it stiff against his neck. It was cold and misting, unusually cold for South Carolina, even if it was December. It reminded him of London, and he did not want to be reminded of London right now. He wanted to think of home. He wanted to think of how the house would smell of his mother's pot roast as soon as he opened the door. She would wipe her hands on her apron and knuckle a tear away from the outside corner of her eye, and it didn't matter how long he had been away, she would expect him to wipe his feet at the door, and this time, he would.

"James," she would say with relief. "James."

His father would come from the kitchen table, folding the newspaper under his arm, and give a firm handshake.

"I told you he'd come home this Christmas," he'd say to his wife without looking at her. He wouldn't want to take his eyes off his son. "Are you okay now, son? Are you okay?" His father would search his eyes for an answer, and seeing one, would say, "Well, you're home now. You're home now, boy. You can rest now."

That's how it would go. Or rather, that's how he hoped it would go.

***

James climbed the narrow steps onto the train and took the first seat available, sliding in against the window. Most people, he had observed, board a train or a bus and keep walking, keep searching for a more desirable seat just ahead and then, never finding one, have to settle for whatever is left near the rear. But James had learned a long time ago that the first offer is usually the best and to take it without hesitation when it comes. After all, it's just human nature to always hope something better is up ahead. That's how so many good things get left behind.

The conductor stopped to clip his ticket and brought a stiff hand to his forehead in a quick salute. "Welcome home, soldier."

James stiffened and returned the salute. He didn't deserve to be saluted and he didn't deserve to return a salute and he didn't deserve to be going home. He didn't deserve the medal pinned to his chest, and he most certainly had not earned the respect offered to him by strangers. As for home, if he was still allowed to call it home, maybe he'd been away long enough that they had all forgotten. Or forgiven.

A man helped a pregnant woman step up onto the train and maneuver down the aisle. With one hand under her round belly, she gave James a nod and a smile. *How do women do that?* he wondered. *How do they walk around with swollen stomachs and with something growing by the hour inside of them for so many months and not be terrified? How do they feel the squirming and nudging and kicking of a life inside of them and not be driven mad with the want of seeing it, to know the color of its eyes and the color and texture of its hair and its gender? How do they sleep at night not knowing whether it is safe and warm or whether it is fighting for its life?* Maybe it was easier to not know. Maybe it was easier to not ask questions and to just keep moving, the same way he did when he hauled a fifty-pound field pack through muddy fields and debris-filled streets, running for his life between falling bombs, or how he slept each night clutching his pack for so many months, pretending to not be terrified.

He looked away, hoping the woman wouldn't sit near him.

A young chaplain boarded the train behind the pregnant woman and caught James's glance.

"Is this seat occupied?" the chaplain asked. His eyes were kind and naive, and his voice was soft and high like a child's.

"Guess not."

"Would you mind?" he gestured to the seat across from James.

"Guess not."

But he did mind. He didn't want to talk to anyone, especially clergy. He didn't want to hear about religion or about God's grace or God's forgiveness or God's plan for his salvation. He had heard enough of that back home.

Home. He could still feel his mother's hand wet from the faucet as she smoothed down the cowlicks on the crown of his head. She straightened his blue-and-brown plaid sport coat and brushed the lint from his trousers as they inevitably ran late for church. His father revved the motor and honked the horn from the driveway.

"He can honk that horn all he wants," she'd say, "but the Lord expects us to look our best for Him now, doesn't He?" She would turn James's head and check for wax in his ears. "Did you see Timothy Spinoli's suit last week in church? It had enough wrinkles in it to make a raisin jealous. I cannot believe Diane let her boy out of the house dressed like that. Well, not me. My little man is going to represent this family with some respect. I know Ben's mother would never let him out looking like he was thrown away. I tell you, James, people these days are losing their respect for so many things. Makes me think the end of days are near. So we better be ready, huh?" She cupped his cheek and kissed the top of his wet head.

James instinctively reached up to smooth his hair but felt the bristle of his military cut and remembered the chaplain sitting across from him. He wanted to be alone. He turned his face to the window, crossed his arms, and vowed not to have a conversation with the child chaplain.

The train released its brakes and lurched forward. James's sangfroid lurched along with it, not sure of what was coming next but deciding that regardless, it would be one inch closer to somewhere else. *Just get home … Just try.*

He watched the palmetto trees pass, and he thought of how silly they looked, jagged and rough and short and providing so little shade or comfort. *How can you even call yourself a tree? More like a bush,* he thought. *A ratty, spiny, useless bush.* And through the fog and mist he saw the gray sliver of an inlet that pointed back to the ocean he had just crossed. What if he had to go back? He wouldn't go back, he averred. He would do anything to not have to go back.

James closed his eyes and leaned his head against the glass and tried to will away the sounds of planes and the bellows of thunder that followed. The shouts. The orders. The panting. The running. The grunting. Trees shaking and leaves shivering and rain and bullets and men falling into the mud. Everywhere, the mud. Marching in mud and sleeping in mud. Trying to dig foxholes in mud, but for every shovelful out, more mud came back in. Boots in mud and faces in mud and men lying in mud not caring if they lived or died. At some point, James no longer cared either.

***

They had been separated from their troop during the last battle and needed to wait for the light of morning to reconvene. They hunched in their makeshift shelter, hands stretched out to catch the slightest warmth from the slightest of fires.

"Jimmy," someone said, "what did you eat today?"

"Haven't," he'd answered. Everything was too much and too long, and he was tired. He wanted to go home. Everyone just wanted to go home.

"Me either. Fellas, we need to eat something," Luther said. Luther was the voice of reason.

"Too tired."

Luther began the laborious task of dragging his muddy pack to his lap to unpack and dig out the C rations. "Come on. We all need to eat."

The others reluctantly followed suit.

"I have a can of steak and mashed potatoes, and chicken and rice. On what shall we dine tonight?" Luther always insisted on being grammatically correct.

They all contributed water that they had collected from a stream earlier in the day and poured it into the small tin pot propped against the flame. They swigged the rest from their canteens, enough to wet their parched tongues until the rest was ready. They waited in silence for the water to boil. The silence was kind at first; it was rest and respite and a prayer and a plea. But it soon became a reality, and the water hissing in the pot grew louder and the distant thunder—always the thunder—and the memories of the day began to scream, and someone had to quell the silence.

"Lost Bill today." Everyone already knew. "Anybody get his tags?"

Michael reached inside his jacket without answering and pulled them out, held them up, dangling. He rubbed the metal imprint respectfully and returned them back to the protection of his inner coat pocket.

"I got Tim's." Luther patted the pocket on his chest.

They spoke of losing friends with no emotion, in the same tone that they would use to report the score of a Yankees game. The ritual was safer that way. It kept things intact, even if it was only for that moment. They didn't bother asking how much longer this madness would last because no one knew the answer, or maybe they were too scared to hear the answer. They didn't bother asking why or for what or how. They only asked for whom. They asked for whom because that was the only answer that they all truly knew, and it was the only answer they needed to know. It was for home. Home.

"Jimmy, what's the first thing you're gonna do when you get home?" Michael asked.

James lifted his bloodshot blue eyes and met Michael's. He despised being called Jimmy. "Not so sure I'm going home."

Luther injected his customary optimism. "Of course you're going home, man. We're all going home. One home may be different from another, but we're all going home, somewhere. Either up there," he pointed skyward, "or right here," he tapped his heart, "or to Mississippi." He smiled thinking of it.

"Tallahassee," Michael said and smiled.

"Where you from, Jimmy?"

"Jersey," Luther answered for him. "Jimmy's from New Jersey. Isn't that right, Jim? The Garden State."

"Guess so," James answered, wanting the conversation about him and about home to end.

"Why do they call it the Garden State? You Yanks got a lot of gardens up there? I don't think of gardens when I think of New Jersey. I think of too many people and cold, murky rivers. And Sinatra. Ole Blue Eyes, they call him. You don't see too many Italians with blue eyes, ya know. Ya think he's really Italian? He might just be sayin' that. Everybody wants to be Italian these days. I'm tellin' ya though, that blue-eyed Italian can sing. Act too. You seen *Ship Ahoy*? My girl loves that movie."

"She doesn't love the movie, moron. She just loves lookin' at Sinatra." Michael jabbed Luther with his elbow and snickered.

James didn't laugh, and he rubbed his hand over the imaginary cowlick on his head.

"Hey, Jim, since you got blue eyes, I'm gonna call you New Blue from New Jersey."

"They got gardens in Jersey, all right. Pansy gardens," Michael winked at Luther, hoping for a rise out of their brooding comrade.

They could read the loathing in his blue eyes, so they left him alone and let him go to wherever his thoughts had taken him. The soldiers fell into the more familiar strategy of telling stories about home and how someone they loved was waiting for them there. Even if the fire didn't warm them, this would.

***

James thought of home, too, and whether he would or wouldn't be welcomed back. He wouldn't blame his parents if they slammed the door and chained the lock as soon as they saw his face. In fact, he wouldn't blame them if they didn't open the door at all. He tried to remember if his parents had a peephole installed in the front door like their neighbors across the street had done.

It used to be that when the front door opened, his mother would immediately stop whatever chore she was doing and kneel down and open her arms for a hug. If he was home from school, she'd ask him about his day. If he was home from a friend's house, she'd ask him what they played and if the other boys were behaving nicely or not. Then she would walk him to the bathroom sink to wash his hands and face and sit him down at the kitchen table for a snack—half of a soda pop poured into a glass and two oatmeal cookies. While he ate and dropped crumbs on the placemat, his mother would set his book bag on the counter to empty his folders, commenting on each gold star and smiley-face sticker as she placed his schoolwork in what she called the "brag basket" on top of the counter. When his father came home from work, he'd give James a firm pat on his back and tousle his hair and say, "Good job, son" and "Proud of ya, kid." Then he'd take his seat in the green cloth recliner and unfold the newspaper tucked under his arm.

Middle school was when James first acknowledged the existence of the opposite sex. He knew they were there, but he didn't know that he was supposed to open doors for them the same way that he had to open doors for his mother and for the older ladies at church. He didn't understand this sudden urge to irritate the same girls that he had avoided for so long on the playground. Now he wanted to throw a ball or a paper airplane at them just to watch their reaction. He wanted to tease them and laugh at them and be around them.

He and his mother were standing at the checkout one afternoon when he recognized Margaret, a girl from the eighth grade. She was carrying a paper bag of canned goods out, and his mother said too loudly, "James, smooth down that cowlick and go open the door for that pretty young lady." He hesitated and looked back to his mother incredulously.

"You heard me, go open the door for her! Hurry!"

"But, Mom, she goes to my school."

"What in the sweet Lord's name does that have to do with anything?" she yelled and caught the attention of everyone nearby. "Go!"

James hesitated again until he felt a smack on the back of his head that made his cowlick bounce back up. He lurched awkwardly toward Margaret and held the door open, his face red and everyone staring at him.

"I know Ben's mother wouldn't have to ask twice for her son to listen to her. What is the matter with you? I thought I raised you to have some manners, young man."

"But she's just a girl at my school," James said, trying to defend himself.

"I don't care if she's a girl from the moon, she's a girl, isn't she? Boys open doors for girls. Period. Chivalry will not go extinct in my household, James David Merritt."

That Sunday, James saw Margaret at church and she and her friends started giggling as soon as they saw him. She held her hand up behind her head like a rooster to tease him about his cowlick. He wasn't quite sure what to do, so he stuck up his middle finger at them like he'd seen a guy do in a movie picture once. The girls were horrified and immediately went and told their parents what James had done. James's father commenced to escort his son out of the sanctuary in front of the entire congregation by the coat collar, dragging him on the tips of his toes. He would never forget that humiliation.

It was a huge relief when James was finally able to sit in the balcony at church. The balcony was the unspoken dominion of the youth, where kids finally had enough freedom to sit somewhere other than under their parents' wingspans in the front pews. In the balcony there was candy, evident by the crackling wrappers of lemon drops and red hots during the sermon and by the trash left behind afterward. John Mills once brought a soda into the balcony and waited until the preacher started a prayer before he popped the top as loudly as he could. They snickered when the preacher paused at the distraction. The girls sat in the balcony too. It was there that James first caught sight of Meredith Malone. She had dark blonde hair and she always wore green dresses that made her eyes look as green as the leaves on a tree. She smelled good too. Like a flower, but he didn't know much about flowers, so he didn't know which one. James was too nervous to speak to her, but his best friend, Ben, wasn't.

"Think she'll like me?" Ben asked James.

"I don't see why not," he answered truthfully.

"Think she'll kiss?"

"How would I know that? Maybe you'll have to try to kiss her to find out," James suggested.

"She's pretty, right?"

"I don't know," James lied. "She's all right, I guess."

"Should I go ask her her name?"

James didn't answer.

"You don't like her, right?" Ben wanted to make sure. "Do you want to ask her instead?"

"No, you go ahead and ask her. I don't care what her name is." He couldn't stop staring at her.

"Yeah, she probably doesn't like guys with cowlicks," Ben laughed and poked James with his elbow. "I'm just kidding. It really isn't that bad. I don't know why it bothers you that much." Ben tried to console him. Just then the girl approached and stood directly in front of them.

"What are you staring at?" She directed the curt question to James.

"Nothing," he stuttered. Her eyes were even greener close up.

"Good. Because I don't like you staring at me." She flipped her hair over her shoulder and started to stomp away.

"Now you've done it," Ben whispered. "Hold on, I'll fix this." Ben straightened his shirt collar and called out, "Excuse me!" The girl turned around.

"I would like to apologize on behalf of my friend here. He has a staring problem and we've been working on it lately. I see that we still have some work to do, so thank you for calling it to our attention. So what's your name?"

"Meredith."

"Meredith?"

"Yes, Meredith Malone. A staring problem isn't the only thing that's wrong with your friend. He also needs a haircut."

"Yes, well, we'll work on that too. I'm Ben. Would you mind if I updated you regularly on my friend's progress?"

Meredith smiled at his game, then tilted her head. "I wouldn't mind, I suppose."

"Great. How 'bout I give you the first update this Friday afternoon right after school? Meet me at the picnic tables by the clock?"

"Sure. I'll bring my notebook to record the data."

"A brilliant idea." Ben returned her smile. He bowed slightly as she turned and walked away.

Ben and James had grown up together, sometimes shared a crib together, their parents joked. They had gone to every school together and tried to be in every class together. They spent summers at each other's houses, and their families went on vacations together. They even snuck their first beer together after discovering an unopened red-and-white aluminum can that had been left behind in the portable metal icebox in his father's garage. They fished the slimy can out of the warm, putrid water and, looking over their shoulders, popped the half-rusted tab and drank it as quickly as they could. It tasted like fetid squirrel piss, they agreed, and they vowed to never, ever drink another beer. They would never be drinking men, they decided that day, and they spit into their hands and shook on it.

Then Ben's parents divorced, and the neighborhood was so shocked at the scandal that they unabashedly shunned the family, and the church folded their arms against them. Ben's father had come home from work early one afternoon and discovered his wife having an affair with a man that lived one street over. The adulterer was also a family man and refused to consider divorce as an option. He opted to pull the brim of his hat down lower over his eyes and lick his wounds instead. Eventually he moved his family away from the abashment and spared them and himself from further humiliation. No one heard from them again. Ben's father left for the city, promising to come back for him once he was settled, but his mother stayed. So Ben came to live with James's family until the ignominy cleared and until he learned enough about forgiveness to finally move back home. It was years before he could bear his mother's embrace again. His father never came back at all.

Ben eventually succeeded in courting Meredith Malone, and they became the most popular couple in school. Meredith was the only thing that Ben ever talked about, and he devoted his life and every teenage thing in it to her. Ben stopped hanging out by the river on the weekends, saying that he'd rather spend his money on his girl instead of hanging around with a bunch of greasy guys. Ben and James stopped going to football games together because Ben only went to the games to watch Meredith cheer with her cheerleading squad, and he sat in the front row so he could be close to her. No more tossing the football in the parking lot, just Meredith. No more cruising for girls on Saturday nights, just Meredith. No more friendship, just Meredith.

James tried to reason with Ben. "You aren't married to her, you know."

"Not yet," he answered with a grin.

"So you're just going to forget all of your friends because of a girl?"

"Listen," Ben explained. "I don't expect you to understand. You don't have a girl. But when you get one, then you'll get it. You'll understand one day, buddy."

James loathed the arrogance of his tone.

So James lost his best friend to the girl they met on the balcony, and it didn't take him long to find out that the wrong crowd had so much more freedom than the right crowd. The "wrong crowd," as his parents called them, never sat on the pews below, and they were allowed to miss church from time to time. Yes, the other crowd had freedom. They sat in cars overlooking the river and could say what they wanted to say without getting a smack to the back of the head. They could sit on the hoods of cars and drink booze and cuss and fist fight and tell dirty jokes and piss on the white walls of their fathers' car tires, and no one could stop them.

At first it was just cigarettes. They were cheap and easy enough to obtain. Everyone smoked cigarettes in the movies, and having a fag hanging from the corner of his mouth made James feel confident and a little like Gary Cooper. His mother always told him he looked like Gary Cooper. He smoothed his hair and practiced the smoldering gaze in the mirror at home more than once, and he liked the look of a cigarette to bolster his image and age.

Cigarettes paired well with a flask of booze, but the booze was harder to come by. James and his buddies preferred the Kentucky whiskey, but it was most often whatever could be confiscated from the backs of their fathers' liquor cabinets. Typical teenage behavior, his parents initially rationalized. It will pass, they hoped. But too many times booze had brought James home in a drunken, drooling rage, and the weekends soon became dreaded events in their household. James would leave the house early on Saturday evening to meet his friends and would come home as someone else. As someone unrecognizable. As someone else's son.

Then James and his buddies experimented with cocaine. The powder was easy to hide in a shoe or a deep pocket and never left an odor on the breath. It only took a thumbnail's worth to feel good instead of a whole bottle, and its effects could be felt immediately. Short and sweet horizons rose in an instant. Best of all, it was nearly undetectable, especially by naive parents. But it was expensive and difficult to obtain. None of James's friends really had the money for it, but as always, the will dictates the way.

Before long, James was stealing money from his mother's pocketbook. He overheard his parents discussing it one night in the living room.

"I just don't understand what happened to it," she told her husband.

"Well I don't either, hon," he answered. "Money doesn't just walk away."

"I think I know that," she snapped. "But do you think someone may have taken it? I did stop by the hardware store earlier today to pick up some bulbs to plant under the kitchen window, and I left my pocketbook at the checkout just long enough to grab a pack of gum from the aisle over. When I went to pay for it, the money was gone. I had to put the bulbs and the gum back. It was humiliating."

In an effort at diversification (a term he had learned in his Economics class), some nights James would wait for his parents to go to bed so he could sneak into the dining room. In the dark, he silently opened the buffet drawer and pulled back the piece of heavy green felt to reveal the silverware. He would slide a couple of spoons and forks or ladles or whatever utensils he could grab into his pockets and hock them the next day for whatever he was offered. When Christmas came and his mother went to set the table for the big family dinner, she sat and cried at the dining room table, knowing exactly what had happened to her silver and exactly what had happened to the money in her purse and exactly what was happening to her only child.

His parents tried restrictions and consequences, but James defied each of them. When they told him he was not allowed to go out on a given night, he simply and amicably agreed with them. Then he went to his room, locked the door, and climbed out of his window. If his father came after him, he'd outrun him. His friends would be waiting down the street to pick him up in someone's car, undoubtedly taken without permission. After he snuck out a few times, they tried locking him in. Mr. Merritt nailed the window shut, so James pulled the chair out from the desk he never used anymore and smashed the window. His parents hurried to repair the window before the neighbors noticed and before they would have to admit what was happening to their family. *James was just playing baseball again*, they'd explain if anyone asked about the broken window.

They tried locking him out once to teach him a lesson, but he only broke the window from the outside in an unstoppable rage when he was tired and hungry and needing to sleep. He had crawled back in through the shattered glass, cutting his hands and legs and not feeling it, leaving a trail of blood that led to the kitchen.

James stumbled home one night and fell against the wall on his way to the kitchen, his shoulder knocking a framed family picture collage off the wall. More shattered glass. His mother hurried from her bedroom and shut the door quickly and quietly behind her. She grabbed her son under the elbow to steady him and walked him to the kitchen table.

"James," she pleaded, "This has to stop. This has to end, do you hear me?"

James scraped his chair back and tried to stand but fell back into the chair instead.

"You're killing yourself, and you are killing this family. Why are you doing this, James? Why?"

He lifted his heavy eyes to meet hers and held them there for a moment. Then he started laughing. He threw his head back and guffawed and choked on his saliva and tried to regain his composure.

"Ma, just ... just shut up, okay?" With his sleeve, he wiped the spit from his chin. "Just go back to bed and leave me alone."

"Leave you alone? How am I supposed to leave you alone? You're my son. I cannot leave you alone."

"Leave me alone!" He shouted and slapped his palm on the table.

"James, be quiet. You're going to wake your father."

"Nothing can wake that old man up." He slapped the table again and again until his mother caught his arms to stop him. He twisted his hands around hers to immobilize her wrists and gripped them too tightly.

"I said, leave me alone." He bared his teeth in a deranged smile and held her gaze.

"James, stop this. Let me go. I don't like the look in your eyes right now." Her voice trembled. His eyes were vacant and hollow, and they stared straight through the tears she held back in her own eyes.

He laughed again at her and shoved her hands away.

"What do we have to eat around here? Got any oatmeal cookies, Ma?" he slurred and tried to stand up. "I'm starving."

"No," she answered stiffly. "Our sugar ration has already been used."

James tore through the pantry shelves and opened the only bag of chips he could find. He crammed a fistful into his mouth and dropped the bag when he found homemade cookies hidden inside a tin. James turned to her.

"Then what is this?"

His mother didn't answer but rushed down the hallway back to the safety of her room and took her Bible into the closet.

The cookie tin lid clanged on the floor and James kicked it out of his way while he went to the fridge for milk. He pulled out the glass carafe and the thick milk sloshed down his cheeks and chin and down the front of his shirt and left a puddle on the floor. He thought of ice cream and unlatched the icebox, spewing profanity and kicking the kitchen chairs when he saw none. The need to sleep finally overcame him, and he teetered back down the hallway and fell onto his bed.

After too many nights like this, James's father finally decided to pull his face out from behind the newspaper and acknowledge the fact that his son was marching down the wrong road and was only steps away from the banks of the Rubicon, and so he did just what his own father had done and put his foot down to reiterate the rules of the household:

Cut your hair. James grew it longer.

Stop using profanity. James cussed louder.

Remember your curfew. James didn't come home.

Respect your mother; you're breaking her heart. James avoided her.

Get a job. James stole.

Go to church. Never again.

One day James came home to the preacher waiting for him in the parlor. He tried to read scripture that applied to the wandering ways of youth and tried to get James to recommit his life to Christ and turn from his sinful ways, but James just stared intently at the preacher in silence until the preacher was so uncomfortable that he left, Bible closed and in hand. "I'll pray for you all," he said and hurried out.

His mother thought herself a modern-day pioneer of the democratic parenting technique, so she wouldn't let her husband lay a hand on James. His father was forced to resort to lecturing, using words like *disappointment* and *ingrate* and *fool*, but James just shoved them aside like the broken glass from his bedroom window. As long as he wore the right shoes, it didn't hurt to walk among sharp words nor shards.

His parents weren't the only ones he had hurt. James began wanting Meredith for himself. She was pretty, James admitted, and smart. She was easy to talk to, and when she tucked her blonde hair behind her ears while she was listening to Ben talk, she looked at Ben with her green eyes in a way that James wanted someone to look at him. So he started wooing her by leaving anonymous notes in her locker. He hurried to beat Ben in being the one to carry her lunch tray and open doors for her. If there was a fight in the hallway, he would grab Meredith's hand and pull her aside to safety, forgetting to let go of her hand when the danger had passed. Ben thought nothing of it at first and even teased James about his newfound chivalry.

James was well aware that he was betraying his best friend and destroying a sacred friendship, but the victory of self was sweeter than the pain of hurting another. For a while, anyway.

Ben said that he could see the dangerous road that James had set out upon, evident by the dark circles under his eyes and the callous gestures that he now used in conversation. He commented on the stench that now followed James in the hallways and on the gait that assumed no purpose or ambition. Ben pulled James aside and tried to warn him about the vile character and motives of the wrong crowd and how their general lack of ambition could become infectious.

James couldn't disagree. Ben was right. It was infectious. But it didn't matter at the time. He wanted something new. Something different. Fresh faces and fresh friends and anything different from his vanilla ice cream family life. And he wanted Meredith.

"What do you think you're doing?" Ben confronted James in the hallway. "Meredith said you've been leaving notes in her locker."

"Is my name on them?"

"No, no one's name is on them. But I know it's you. She knows it's you."

"Maybe it is and maybe it isn't. She likes them, though, doesn't she?" James grinned slowly and bore his eyes into Ben's. "Doesn't she."

Ben cocked his arm and started to swing but James caught his wrist and undercut him with a punch to the gut. Ben doubled over and clenched his stomach.

"No need to bow down to me, Benny boy," James said and shoved Ben's head against the metal lockers. Meredith heard the commotion and ran toward them.

"Your boyfriend here took a swing at me," James explained. "He missed. Let me know when you're ready for a real man, Mere. I'll be waiting for you. I'll spend my whole life waiting for you." He softened his gaze to quell the trepidation in her eyes.

"You have become a miserable excuse for a human being." Those were the last words Ben ever spoke to him.

"Guess so."

James eventually convinced Meredith to give him a chance. Ben had conceded to exist in the comfort of mediocrity, the bane of every teenage boy, while James was more exciting, more fun, more adventurous. His locker notes became bolder, his bravado more evident, and he swooped in with big words and big deeds and won Meredith over. Then he impregnated her to seal the victory. The crown of his conquest. A final spear in the side of the righteously spoken.

When Meredith told James she was pregnant and that she didn't know what to do, he smirked and mumbled something about Ben. She wanted to talk about it, to discuss how they were going to tell their parents, to hear him tell her he was going to be a good father and that she'd be a good mother and they would be a happy family. Instead, he left her standing on the sidewalk with fear and regret etched on her face. He rode off with his friends to the river.

That Saturday night Meredith showed up at the river in her father's car. The headlights bounced up and down on the dirt road as she pulled up next to the group of parked cars. Her eyes immediately landed on James with his white T-shirt that was filthy and torn. His disheveled dark hair was pushed back off his forehead to reveal a cut above his arched brow; dried blood and dried leaves were stuck in his hair. He squinted his eyes against the lights and saw Meredith's gaze drop to the glass bottle in his hand. She had never seen him like this—never seen him at the river. She knew he would harmlessly drink beer with the guys sometimes, but he recognized the look of shock on her face. This was different; he was different. He set his shoulders back and approached the hood of her car.

"What are you doing here? What the hell are you doing here?" He banged his fist on the hood.

"I came to find you. I just wanted to talk about things ... I thought we could just talk," she stammered.

James wiped his runny nose on his bare arm and took a slug from the bottle.

Rage ensued.

"Get the hell out of here!" he yelled at her. He waved his arms and pointed back to the main road. "Go!"

"What is wrong with you? Why are you acting like this?"

He stepped around to the car door. "We don't have anything to talk about."

"I don't understand. What do you expect me to do?"

James's friends were laughing in the background, and one of them smashed a bottle against the rocks. The river was quiet, drowned out by the sounds of teenagers trying to convince themselves that they were old enough to do as they please.

"You do whatever you want to do," he said coldly.

"Whatever I want? You did this, James." She pointed to her stomach. "You did this. We did this."

Someone called for James from the throng of guys sitting on car hoods. He waved them off.

"Listen, I don't want to be a father and I don't want to be a husband and I don't want you snooping around to see what I'm doing. You need to leave."

"Jamey, listen to me." Meredith was crying now. She was out of the car and grabbed his arms to try to hold him still. "We can do this, okay? We'll be graduating soon, and you can stop this nonsense and clean yourself up. You can find a job and we can rent a little apartment. I can get a job at the market to help you, and we could raise our beautiful baby and be a family. We could save up for a house and we could be so happy. We have to do this! If you leave me, my parents will send me away to live with my aunt and they'll never speak to me again. You know my dad; he'll do it. He won't ever speak to me again. Jamey, please. We can do this. We can make this work. Please," she sobbed and reached her arms up around his neck.

"Hey, James, we got a line over here waiting for you! Get rid of that kitten and get back over here or that line's gonna be mine!" The hoarse voice came from a booze-soaked boy.

"Coming," he answered laughing as he unclasped her hands from his neck and pushed her back into the car.

"I love you, Jamey," she said, desperate to keep him there. "Don't leave."

He took another pull from the bottle and coughed.

"What about the baby?"

"Do what you want."

"This isn't you. That's the liquor talking. You said you loved me. You said you'd do anything to have me. Well, now you have me."

"You're a fool. I don't love you. It was a game, and I won. I won the prize." He held the bottle up like a trophy. "Maybe Ben will take care of your baby." He meant for it to hurt her, but he didn't know why.

"It's our baby. And I don't want Ben. I chose you, remember? Although sometimes I wonder why. Like right now."

"Leave," he commanded.

"No, not without you. Come with me."

"Leave!" He clenched his fist and threw his head back and screamed as he slammed the glass bottle against the car door. "I won, and I'm done."

He stumbled back to his friends, and they clapped him on the back. He looked back over his shoulder to make sure Meredith was watching him as he leaned over the hood of a car and put his finger to the side of his nose.

The dark road James staggered on got darker and deeper until soon it was an unwieldy bog that sucked him down and kept him wallowing in a quagmire of disillusion and helplessness. James brazenly went back to stealing from his mother's purse, even the coins that had wedged themselves in the creases of the seams. He stole the hidden roll of bills from the back corner of his father's sock drawer, and he took the remainder of the silverware from the buffet. Then one day he started walking. He walked away without goodbyes and without tears or love or desire or goodness. Save the pelf stuffed in his pockets, he was empty. He looked behind him one last time, though he knew there would be no one coming after him this time. He knew his father would be consoling his sobbing mother as they watched his silhouette fade down the road. James had chosen this life, and he knew his parents were tired of chasing him and tired of trying to save him. Their door would forever be closed and locked.

The life he chose was grand at first. He was invited to stay at a friend's house rent free until he could get a job and find a place of his own. It was a new freedom, not having to argue with his parents every time he stepped in or out of the door. He could eat whenever and whatever he wanted with whomever he wanted. He didn't have to worry about Meredith looking over his shoulder and judging the decisions he made. He could sleep late and come home late and never had to endure seeing the disappointment on his parents' faces nor in Meredith's eyes. Those eyes, he remembered, then willed them away. But the money went fast. His friend's father soon discovered the drugs and alcohol and kicked James out and sent his own son to West Point on the favor of a family friend.

James slept on a park bench for several nights, determined to not crawl back home in defeat. Home was too far away now. So without money or cocaine or liquor, his body shivered from the deficiency and all night from the cold. The bench he chose was hidden behind a row of peony bushes with a plaque commemorating the local ladies' Garden Club. The surrounding area was mulched with wood chips that he could smell on a breeze from time to time, and a border of white rocks that seemed to have a light of their own under the streetlamp at night. No one knew he was there. He wandered during the day, mimicking the gait of someone with importance and intention, but as soon as darkness fell and people went home to their warm houses and families, he collapsed on his bench, his feet aching from the day's deception. He lay huddled under discarded pages of the *Jersey Journal* that he had discreetly collected during the day and tucked under his arm like his father.

His body demanded sleep, but his mind haunted him with visions of drink and cocaine and the river. He thought of his parents and wondered how they were coping without him—probably much better, he decided. He thought of Meredith, and a hot, sickening feeling swarmed in his stomach. He wondered what she decided and whether he was going to be a father or not. Did she really love him, or did she just love the idea of being loved? Did he love her? No. Maybe. And he thought of Ben. James had skipped graduation, and he remembered the plans that he and Ben had made since middle school to walk across the stage wearing only boxer shorts beneath their robes.

When James couldn't sleep, he read whatever article was closest to his face. By the light of streetlamp and matches, he learned about things greater than himself for the first time. Women were playing professional softball on Wrigley Field. Eighteen million women were working in factories to help with the war. The Steelers and Eagles had merged to become the Pennsylvania Steagles because so many players had been drafted. PT-109 was sunk by a Japanese destroyer; Lieutenant John F. Kennedy survived. U-boats were tracked offshore in the Atlantic. US General Dwight D. Eisenhower was named supreme Allied commander. Rations were enacted on rubber-soled shoes, canned goods, meats, cheeses, butter, cooking oils.

James knew the war was in full swing, but he never cared to learn the where or why. He was suddenly fascinated by the concept of a soldier, something he had never considered before. He saw photographs of soldiers standing together, their countenances sober and sure, and something in him wanted to be standing there alongside them.

A realization was taking shape among the shadows that hovered beneath the streetlamps. Maybe he had been too preoccupied with trying to prove a point that was never meant to be proven. Maybe he had been so consumed with trying to be somebody that he became nobody. He inexplicably wanted to read his own name in print now. Something was growing in him, and it was fascinating and frightening and fulfilling, and he wanted it. He wanted to be a part of this thing, of anything, really, where men were allowed to be heroes, no matter where they came from or what they had done. The idea of anonymity felt cathartic. One man in a sea of men swaying the tide of victory. One ripple on a pond, one stripe on a tiger, one granule of sand on a beach, guarding the shore. That's what he wanted. And so when the first light hit the tops of the trees the next morning, he tucked the cluttered, worn paper back under his arm and hitchhiked his way to the nearest recruitment office in Trenton. Each time a car slowed and pulled over, all James had to say was that he was going to join the army to fight Hitler, and the driver would immediately open his door and pat him on the back. He was called "a fine young man," and he was talked to like a man, and he was all of a sudden proud of something before he had even accomplished it.

* * *

"I wish we were back in London," Michael said, pulling James back from his reverie. The rain pelted the scant tarp in intermittent showers, helping them avoid the apprehension of silence. Thunder echoed in low decibels, spreading like a heavy quilt over a feverish child, and bursts of light flickered through the trees in the distance. The chill in the rain had settled in on their psyches.

"Me too," Luther agreed. "The Brits are good to us."

"They shouldn't be," Michael argued.

"Why not?"

"Because we beat 'em. In the Revolution. If you think about it, they ought to hate our guts."

Luther laughed. "You're right. I suppose they ought to. Maybe they're just glad to be rid of the likes of us scalawags. Or maybe they need us. Either that," Luther paused and added a broken twig to their spartan fire, "or maybe they've just plain forgiven us. Forgiveness, my boys, is a beautiful thing."

James considered the words and then dismissed them like folklore. *Forgiveness doesn't exist. Not truly,* he thought to himself. *People can say they forgive you all they want, but if it can't be forgotten, then it can't be forgiven. No one truly forgives. It's just a comforting word for a fool to hold on to.*

James recalled the training video that the troops were made to watch before their deployment to London. Don't be loud in the pubs. Don't brag. Don't get drunk. Learn to play darts. Learn to drink tea. Learn to drink warm beer. Don't discuss wages. Don't ogle the women. Be respectful of people's homes and their rations. Don't be a glutton. Wear tags at all times. Look neat at all times.

When the bombs started falling, Londoners appeared on their balconies and at their front doors to peer out at the spectacle. Heavy planes flew low to drop their loads and veered up and away before the reverberations could be felt. James and the other soldiers would yell for the people to get back inside, take cover, but some of them couldn't take their eyes off the fireworks, and the accompaniment of deep bass booms bellowed for two days. The reemergence of fear had many mesmerized by the wide swath of searchlights scanning the skies for the bellies of bombers, and remembering the Blitz, they rushed to collect pieces of shrapnel and historic edifice rubble to keep as souvenirs. Soon after, James's troop was sent to Germany for the squeeze.

And here they were. Running like mice through a field and hiding behind anything that stood taller than they did or was sunken lower. Ditches, trees, barns, dead animals, dead men. Anything. Anything to try to make it home.

"Sometimes I think it'd be easier to just give up," Michael whispered.

James had thought of that too. They all had.

"No way, champ," Luther answered. "If we give up, then all of this would be for nothing. All of it. All of this would've just been a waste of time. No way. We can't give up."

Just then the tarp ripped open, and a thud threw Luther back against his pack. His eyes were stunned wide open, and he grabbed his neck where the blood arced out like a silent Parisian fountain.

"Luther!" Michael yelled and scrambled for his rifle. He fell on top of Luther to guard him against more gunfire and shouted for James to get a tourniquet. Michael fired into the darkness. "Hurry up! Wrap him up!"

James heard another shot and saw the tarp blistered to shreds, and he rolled sideways out of the shelter and started running. He couldn't see in the dark and didn't know where he was going. He didn't care where he was going as long as he got away. He could hear Michael screaming, his voice high and desperate and demented, and James kept running until he couldn't hear the voices anymore.

He sat at the base of a tree, covered in mud and leaves and shame, and considered his next move. He had left his pack behind in the shelter. He had to go back. But not now. Not now. He couldn't go back now.

He waited for dawn, shivering and shaken, and retraced his steps back to the shelter. He searched the trees for a possible locale where the enemy may still be hidden, waiting for him, and realizing that the shots could come from any direction, he crouched behind the dead bodies of Michael and Luther. They had both been shot—Luther in the neck and Michael in the head. Both died with their eyes wide open. He wondered about the last thing they'd seen. Angels? Demons? Their families? A swastika on a sleeve? James positioned their bodies like a shield in front of him and was grateful that he hadn't allowed himself to grow close to either of them. Troops would be along soon, he reasoned. Reinforcement would be here soon. He braced his rifle over the shoulder of a dead man and poised his finger on the trigger.

Troops arrived three days later, and a coward was made a hero. James explained what happened: We got separated from our troop, it got dark, so we made camp to stay put till morning. We were talking, boiling water and getting ready to eat; gunshots from I don't know where ... two soldiers dead. I used them as protection while I returned fire. I don't know if I hit them ... Enemy retreated, I guess. No more shots fired.

***

The chaplain watched James sleep. He watched his feet twitch and saw his face contort into emotions that didn't have names. His face was clean and young, maybe late teens, early twenties, he calculated, and his dark brown hair would soon need another trim to meet requirements. His hands were twisted and holding something so dear that he obviously didn't want to let go. A gun? A hand? A hope? He felt sorry for the soldier, but he wasn't sure why. He saw the medal of valor on his jacket and thought he must have done something good and brave and heroic in the war, and he was probably going home for Christmas on a well-deserved furlough. He wondered where. He imagined who would be waiting for him, though he saw no wedding band. He looked for a name on his bag or lapel but saw none. Then he felt a sudden urge to pray for him. The chaplain kept his eyes open as he prayed, not understanding and not wanting to look away from this enigma of a man, and prayed for he knew not what.

Chapter Two

Exhale and breathe, exhale and breathe,
And I will do the same.
Drag your soul up through your throat,
And purge the Coward's name.
Sneak and slide, then rise and bide
Past mores and fear and shame,
Then stand and speak and know thyself—
God, keep me on this train.

Eleanor McCollum Vaillant boarded the train in Charleston and walked toward an empty seat at the back of the car. She glanced quickly at the soldier and the young chaplain seated by the door as she passed, then fixed her eyes intently forward. Her soft, manicured hands touched the corners of the vinyl seats one by one, part balance, part propeller. Her light-brown hair caught the waning daylight in a dull slant, then curled just under her jawline. Her eyes were brown and deep and quiet, and while her makeup was simple, her somber lips were stained a dark burgundy. She needed to get to that seat before her trembling legs betrayed her and spilled her into the floor in a pathetic scene. She needed to sit down and grab a hold of herself and sort this out. What would her parents say? What would her friends say? What would Christopher say? She hurried into her seat and immediately placed her purse in the seat beside her to discourage another passenger from sitting there. The wedding band on her slender finger was loose, and she spun it around and around nervously with her thumb.

Ellie was eighteen years old and only one day married. She met her husband, Captain Christopher Vaillant, when she was a senior in high school, and he was just the handsome, debonair beau that her parents had always planned for her. He was a Citadel graduate, and he shot up through the ranks in the army like a bullet out of his own obsessively cleaned rifle.

It was clear that Ellie would make a good housewife. Her mother saw to it that both of her daughters learned the art of proper homemaking. She knew how to host tea parties and afternoon socials with silver trays full of teacakes and pimiento cheese sandwiches cut into tiny triangles. She could make a lemon pound cake and spread the slices out like a decorative Chinese hand fan, and she mastered the exact ratio of sugar to hot water and tea and cubes of ice for the perfect glass of sweet tea. She knew how to daintily offer her hand, gloved or not, to a gentleman, respectfully but not flirtingly, and she knew how to wear a hat with a bright feather without looking like a vaudeville floozy. She knew how to hold a conversation with the elites of Charleston and how to conduct herself accordingly in all manners of society.

But she didn't like having to do any of it.

After graduation, Ellie always thought she might attend St. Mary's College, not as a pathway to a certain lofty career and not to tilt the hats of any particular occupation askew, but to be the first female in her family to have a college education. But then Christopher stepped into her life, and Christopher disagreed. He insisted that, as his wife, she would never need to work and thereby would have no need for a college degree. He would provide for her, he bragged, because he was taught that if a woman ever had to go to work, it was only because her husband had failed in his duty. If a woman chose to work, it was because she was dissatisfied with her home life. A dissatisfied housewife makes a poor mother. A poor mother raises poor children.

Poor children make poor decisions that could ruin a family's good name. And so the cycle goes, and therefore he would not have his wife joining the fast-rising ranks of working women. Besides, he reasoned, he would be away from home for much of the war, and she would need to stay home and care for the several children he hoped to produce.

At first, Ellie bristled at this philosophy, but eventually she understood this reasoning since she, too, had hopes of starting a family someday. So she temporarily shelved her college aspirations and focused on the truer reason for wanting to be married: to escape.

Ellie lived a privileged life, and her family had largely been untouched by the ruthless grip of the Depression. Many of her friends' families, however, had been devastated by it and were still trying to recover years later. It embarrassed Ellie for her father to pick her up from school in his shiny black Ford Coupe, while other students had to walk long distances in shoes that didn't fit their feet. As soon as Ellie outgrew something in size or fondness, she would secretly gift it to her closest friends like contraband. Dresses, shirts, shoes, bras, slips, even hats would be smuggled out of her house and gifted to those whose needs they met. If her mother asked her about a certain article of clothing that she had not seen Ellie wear in a while, Ellie would simply explain that it had been torn or damaged or misplaced, and the matter was quickly dismissed as trivial.

At the height of the Depression, Ellie remembered telling her parents how she'd like to help her friends, but they insisted that they needed to take care of their own and couldn't be bothered worrying about everyone else. It was enough, they believed, that Queenie, their housekeeper, had not been let go, while most of the other help was being dismissed as often as thunderstorms in August.

"We'll be okay, but the Yanks are the ones that ought to be worried about the Depression," Ellie's father had chimed in. His cigar moved up and down with his mouth as he spoke. "They don't know how to do anything that doesn't revolve around the almighty dollar and the Open and Closed signs hangin' on a door. Down here we know how to grow things worth growing. Sure they have the steel plants and the production lines and the factories, but you ever tried to eat steel?

You ever gnawed on a piece of rubber and been satisfied? No, sir. The South won't ever go hungry. We might be poor, we might not have the nicest china on the dinner table, but at least we got good food on our plates. Those big city Yanks are crammed up together tight as pages in a book and can't figure out why there aren't enough jobs and food for all of 'em. And they call us stupid. Well, I beg to differ."

Ellie's aspirations to help feed the poverty-stricken in Charleston began at an early age. She used to sneak bowls of soup up to her bedroom where she had lined up her dolls on the floor and spooned soup into each of their porcelain mouths. The springer spaniel named Sumter would help with the drippings and cleanup, while Ellie's older sister, Elisabeth, threatened to tattle if she didn't do certain chores for her.

"Mother's gonna kill you, Ellie," she'd say with a sneer.

"But they're hungry."

"You'll be hungry, too, if Mother catches you wasting soup on your stupid baby dolls. And you're spilling it all over their outfits."

"They aren't stupid. They're just hungry, and I can share my soup."

"Well when you're done spilling soup everywhere, you better come and clean my shoes for church tomorrow."

"Why do I have to do it?" Ellie questioned.

"Because if you don't, I'm telling Mother that you're up here making a mess. You know you aren't supposed to have food up here anyway."

At school, Ellie would share her lunch with the children who stared at her sandwiches and elaborately cut fruit. Queenie took great care to cut Ellie's fruit into shapes of stars and hearts and letters. The kids would gather around each day to see what Ellie brought for lunch, and she inevitably gave it all away.

In high school she thrived in horticulture and became intrigued with small-scale farming. Most of her father's friends were rice and tea and cotton farmers, so she found herself lingering at the dinner table long after the meal was finished to glean any knowledge she could from their conversations about crops and new harvesting techniques.

Ellie made sketches of the garden that she wanted to plant. She would grow collards and squash and corn and beans and tomatoes and okra and cucumbers and cantaloupes and watermelons. She factored in the cost of the seeds and the time and seasons and soil types needed. She planned to set up a table at the end of Church Street every morning and give her harvest away to the needy. But again, Ellie's plans and pleas fell on the deaf ears of her parents. Her father called her naive. He called it a pipe dream and said that she could never grow enough to feed them all and that people would fight over the slim rations and thereby cause more problems than those that already existed. Though he had plenty of both, he refused her the acreage and the money for the seedlings. Her mother told her she needed to bandage her bleeding heart if she was going to survive in this world.

So Ellie turned to the kitchen, where her father had no jurisdiction. Queenie patiently taught her how to make beautiful pies and fruit-filled cobblers, and Ellie's mother was proud that her daughter was learning the skills to make a good housewife. Ellie baked pies every day, and for every pie or cobbler that she made for her family, she made five more to give away. She hid them in different places while they cooled so her mother wouldn't question the quantity and delivered them to strangers as they walked by her house. Soon, the foot traffic outside their black iron gate had noticeably increased. Some pedestrians lingered, some passed by back and forth several times in a short period of time, and some were so bold that they stopped and leaned against the lamppost and gazed out at the Battery until there was a tap on their elbow and a pie appeared. Ellie's father noticed the increase in pedestrians in their immediate vicinity and began holding vigil in his rocking chair on the front porch, determined to discern the cause of the unusual commotion.

"It's like a circus out there," he reported to his wife. "Where are these people coming from all of a sudden? Where are they going? And why do they have to walk by my house to get there?" He puffed out his cigar smoke in short, quick bursts to demonstrate his aggravation. When the rocking chair proved an inefficient perch, he took to leaning against the porch columns or on the porch rail and leering at the passersby until eventually his presence on the porch was so intimidating that the pie pedestrians gathered instead at the street corner at the end of the block and out of sight of the McCollum house.

One day Ellie was carrying a warm blueberry cobbler and noticed a family coming out of the grocery store. The mother was wearing a work dress and struggled to balance a baby on one hip while holding a small bag and another child's hand, using her hip to open the door. A third child trailed behind. Ellie approached them with the cobbler.

"Excuse me, ma'am?" She tried to hold the door open for her. The woman looked at Ellie but didn't answer. "Are these your children?" She knew it was a ridiculous question, but she didn't know how else to start the conversation. Not everyone was open to charity, she had learned. Some people considered kindness an insult.

"Why is that your bus'ness?" The woman snapped. "Have they done somethin' wrong? They didn't steal nothin'."

"Oh, no, ma'am. I wasn't insinuating that at all. I was just wondering if they like blueberry cobbler?"

"Like what?"

"Blueberry cobbler. I just made a fresh one, and I'd be happy to give it to you and your family." Ellie lifted the tin plate in her hand and peeled back the cloth so the children could see and smell the cobbler. The children's eyes grew wide as they looked at the cobbler and then up at their mother for permission.

"Lady," the mother responded, "I don't know who you are or what you tryin' to do here, but I ain't fallen outta the back of no turnip truck. I got no idea what you put in that thing, and I ain't feedin' my babies nothin' that didn't come from my own kitchen. Now 'scuse me." The woman pulled her children away and hurried down the street.

"I love blueberry cobbler," said a voice from behind. Ellie turned and saw a young man in a cadet uniform, his cheekbones sharp and clean and his hair shaved on the sides and parted neatly to the left on the top. He smiled and his lips were thin and tight; his teeth were straight and white.

"Well, then you can have it," Ellie answered as she handed over the cobbler. "She certainly didn't want it."

"No, she didn't," he agreed. "But you have to admit, it's a little unusual for a pretty girl to be walking around Charleston offering hot blueberry cobblers to strangers."

"You're a stranger, and you accepted it."

"Good point. I'm Christopher Vaillant," he introduced himself and bowed slightly. "Now, there, I'm not a stranger anymore." He smiled warmly. "And I'm assuming that since this cobbler is still warm, you live somewhere in this vicinity. May I walk you home?"

And thus their courtship began. Ellie was smitten over the handsome guy who gave her all of his attention. When she spoke, he listened and let her talk as long as she liked. He came to visit her almost every evening, and they would sit in the front porch rockers with glasses of sweet tea and a slice of pie between them. As she talked, she noticed him staring at her, calculating, assessing, and his eyes always rested on her mouth. It disconcerted her initially, but when she mentioned the unnerving behavior to her sister, her sister said it was because he was sizing her up to see if she'd make him a good wife.

"You better not let go of this one," her sister warned her. "You might not get this lucky again."

Christopher demanded respect and doled out respect in return. He removed his hat before he shook her father's hand, and he looked him in the eye. He never stepped on the McCollum porch without flowers for both Ellie and her mother. He was a regular guest at the McCollum house for dinner.

"His table manners are immaculate," her mother said. "He must have been raised in a fine family."

Ellie finally grew comfortable enough to tell Christopher about her dream to have a produce garden one day so she could help feed the needy, and that she had an idea to open a bakery to sell her pies and cobblers, and that whatever didn't sell that day could be donated to the poor. "And why," she wondered aloud to him, "don't restaurants do that anyway?" He rarely answered her; he just smiled and cupped her chin in his palm and told her that her cause was noble and kind.

"Do you think I'm pretty?" Ellie asked him one day. "Mother says I'm average." She spun the yellow jonquil that he brought her between her fingers and put it to her nose.

"Of course I think you're pretty."

"Do you think I'm beautiful?"

"I think you're pretty," he repeated.

"Pretty but not beautiful? I'd rather be beautiful."

"Well, you're pretty. You're not beautiful. But you see, I don't want a beautiful girl. If I had a beautiful girl, I'd have to worry about every Tom, Dick, and Harry fawning over her and then her liking the attention. I'd have to shoot every man that came to the house, and I'd never be able to let her out of my sight. You can't trust beautiful, and that won't work in my line of business. But pretty, on the other hand, means I get a pleasant view without the hassle."

She wasn't sure if she should be offended or not; she guessed she understood what he meant and why, but it didn't feel quite right. So she took her thoughts back to her garden and the promise Christopher gave her that he would give her one someday.

Months passed and the weather quickly grew hot and humid. Ellie walked across the school auditorium stage to claim her diploma, and Christopher sat alongside her parents. He applauded and put his fingers to the corners of his mouth to whistle when her name was called. It was a source of pride for Ellie to have such a handsome man in uniform waiting for her with a bouquet of flowers, and she lingered so her friends could see them together.

"I graduated from the Citadel on the dean's list with first honors in the Corp of Cadets," Christopher boasted to Ellie's parents one evening over dinner. "But as you know, I'm originally from Arkansas."

"Arkansas," Mr. McCollum echoed, disregarding the other accolade. "What's in Arkansas? Is that even a real state?"

He joked, but Christopher wasn't amused.

"Indeed it is, sir. One of the best, I'd wager. We have excellent game hunting and fishing, expansive farmlands, and I believe us to be one of the most patriotic states in our country. In fact, my father just sent word that Arkansas has received about twenty-three thousand

German and Italian prisoners of war. We were one of the few states chosen to house camps and installments to help with the war efforts."

"Now that you've finished at the Citadel, I assume that means your time in South Carolina has come to an end. Do you intend to return to Arkansas?" Mr. McCollum asked, not bothering to hide his intent.

Christopher turned to look at Ellie. "That depends," he said. "I've been looking for the opportunity to tell you all this, and it seems now's the time. I've received my orders for deployment."

Ellie quietly placed her fork down on the rim of her plate and reached for the cloth napkin on her lap. She dabbed at her mouth to conceal her shock, but her mother did not.

"Oh no! Christopher! That's terrible news!" she said. "Do you know how many people are dying over there every single day?" Her hysteria heightened. "What if you get shot by those awful Germans and die?"

"Mrs. McCollum," he said, trying to console her. "This is what I signed up for. I've been training for this, and I assure you, I have been trained very well. It's an honor for me to serve our nation. I'm actually looking forward to it, save one small detail." He looked at Ellie again. "I would like to have something to come home to." He reached inside his starched uniform jacket and pulled out a small box. "With your permission, sir," he nodded to Ellie's father, "I would like to ask for your daughter's hand in marriage." He pushed out his chair and descended to his knee while he opened the box and presented the diamond ring to Ellie. She looked at her mother, who had tears springing from her wide eyes, and she looked at her father, whose hand was rubbing his forehead. He nodded his approval but exhibited no signs of happiness.

Ellie looked around the dining room, annoyed at the perfectly placed silverware and glasses and linen tablecloth. She looked at the rose-colored floral curtains that framed the wavy glass panes from ceiling to floor, and she looked at the busy Oriental rug that had been shipped from wherever her mother had demanded. Her mother's hands were clasped over her mouth, waiting for Ellie to answer. Her father looked away. Then she thought of a garden, of pies and cobblers, and freedom.

"I accept." Ellie extended her ring finger to Christopher.

She would be glad to be out of the house and chart her own direction. Her mother was likewise thrilled with the proposal and insisted the wedding be held at their home under manicured magnolias and views overlooking the Battery. It would have to happen quickly; Christopher's deployment was to take place in one week. So the engagement was announced on Tuesday, the invitations were telegrammed on Wednesday, and the wedding was scheduled for December 14.

Ellie's mother went into five-star general mode. "The magnolias won't be in bloom, but there's nothing we can do about that. We'll need to see that the lawn is groomed to perfection. You don't want the grass to be too high because your shoes may sink too far and make your bridal gait awkward. But not too short because short grass is sparse and tacky. With any luck, the camellias will bloom, and Ell? What kind of flowers do you want to carry? I think lilies would be perfect. Yes, we'll have lilies. They'll match Mother's gown best. I'll need to see if any florists have any this time of year. We've got to set a menu as well. I'm thinking light fare because I don't feel like I should be responsible for feeding a whole passel of Christopher's cadet friends, and I don't even know his family or what kinds of things they eat in Arkansas. Chairs. We need to get chairs, and we need to have the gazebo repainted. It hasn't been done in years." She jotted another line on her lengthening list.

Ellie tried to protest the tradition of having to wear her grandmother's wedding dress. It was neck high in lace with frilly scalloped edging, and the age of the dress had dulled its original ivory to a buttercream color.

"Tradition trumps fashion," her mother reminded her when Ellie suggested that they should remove the veil and shorten the length.

Christopher was promoted to captain just before the wedding, and the promotion required a transfer to Fort Bragg, North Carolina. He would be provided with a house on the base, a small, respectable brick ranch that was located within the officers' cul-de-sac neighborhood.

"What's North Carolina like?" Ellie asked after Christopher told her that they'd be relocating immediately after the wedding. They strolled down the waterfront, listening to the water lap against the seawall below them. The wind was cool coming off the water this time of year. She buttoned the top button of her camel-colored wool coat and tied the sash tighter around her waist. "I've never been out of Charleston."

"Well, if you're expecting Bragg to be like Charleston, it's not. Not even close. No place is like Charleston. But does it really matter? It's going to be our home, and it'll be where we start our family."

Her mind veered to how much she hated the plain white curtains in her bedroom at home. Her mother picked them out to match the plain white quilt on her bed.

"White goes with everything," she always insisted. "It's clean and fresh and it's practical."

Ellie was elated to imagine that soon she would be free to choose whatever color curtains and quilts she liked. She could choose her own dishes and linens and tablecloths and decorative pillows. She could hang whatever kind of wallpaper she wanted and paint the window shutters red if she so pleased. She gripped Christopher's arm a little tighter to retain her excitement.

"Is there a yard for my garden?" She beamed up at him.

"Most houses have yards," he answered sarcastically.

"A kitchen?"

"And most houses have kitchens."

"Good. That's all I need. Then I can bake as many pies and cobblers as I want."

He smirked. "Just like a woman. You have no idea how the world works, but you think baking a pie is going to solve all the world's problems. You should bake Hitler or Tojo a pie. Maybe that'll convince them that they're wrong, and they'll call the war off just for you."

She recognized the patronization. She'd heard it sneak past his lips several times lately.

"I just feel like if there is something I can do, even if it's just a pie for someone, then I should do it. I should at least try to help. I won't apologize for that." She turned to watch the gulls swirl around the church steeple down the street.

"Chris, are you scared to go?" She wanted to change the subject.

He stopped suddenly and darted his eyes at her. "Don't ever call me Chris. That isn't my name. My father named me Christopher, and that's what I'll answer to. My mother tried shortening my name to Chris when I was a baby, and my father popped her in the mouth. She couldn't talk through her swollen lips for a week. My name is Christopher."

Ellie said nothing, but something twisted in her stomach. Christopher resumed walking and sensed her hesitancy. He pulled her hands into his and rubbed them warm. He kissed her knuckles to calm her.

"But am I scared of going overseas? Scared of war?" he asked, returning to the conversation. "Not at all. Fear, my dear, is for women and children."

"Well, I'm not scared either," she lied, tilting her chin up. "I'm ready to be far from this place and I'm ready to be married and I'm ready to start living my life the way I want to. I'm sick and tired of being told what to do and what to wear and how to act."

"Do I have a troublemaker on my hands?" he chided her. He put his arm around her small shoulders and gave her a little squeeze. "How 'bout you just be what you're supposed to be and the world will stay aright. Bad things only happen when people try to change things that've always worked perfectly fine before."

"I thought that was called progress," she challenged.

"You can progress yourself down the aisle and become my wife. That's all you need to do."

The conversation was over. The first red flag had been unfurled.

Still, she wanted to get out of Charleston. She wanted to see and be and do. She would walk down the aisle and take her chances with this captain who would pry her out from behind the caging bars of her parents' home and take her away from here. *Escape.*

The days before the wedding were a frantic, worrisome mess, and she had not heard from Christopher for several days. Finally, late on the eve of their wedding, he stumbled up the front steps to the porch and banged on the door. His eyes were bloodshot, and his face was several days unshaven. He invited himself into the foyer.

"Good evening, my dear." He tried to bow but lost his balance and skipped to one side. "I suppose I'll be seeing you tomorrow," he cupped his hand under her chin.

"Where have you been? You reek." She pulled away from his face to avoid his sour liquor breath.

"Sowing oats, my bride. I'm getting ready to be a married man, you know."

"What exactly does 'sowing oats' entail?" she asked, but she already knew. She could smell the perfume and booze on his uncharacteristically disheveled clothes.

"No, no, no, little girl," he chided her and waved his finger in her face. "That's not your business just yet, my love. After we say our vows, I'm all yours, Ellie McCollum-almost-Vaillant. But until then, I'll not be made to answer to anyone."

"You should get some sleep," she said curtly and escorted him to the door.

If it wasn't already too late, she'd have broken off the engagement on the porch that night. But it was too late. Her parents had too much invested in the wedding, and guests were already on their way. She tried to remember that he would soon be deployed and then she could do as she pleased. She had a house to call her own now, she reminded herself, and she'd be busy decorating it with her own style and personality. Then when Christopher came home, he would be impressed with everything that she'd done, and he will have missed her terribly, and then he'll be the good man she hoped he would be. *We'll be fine*, she consoled herself. *Just a few kinks to work out, and we'll be fine. He's financial security, and he's my ticket out of Charleston.*

The wedding was simple but beautiful. The magnolia trees had been decorated in ribbons and bows. The camellias had indeed bloomed after a mild frost and dotted the perennial green backdrop in white and purple and pink. White wooden chairs were perfectly lined in the measured and mowed lawn, and the freshly painted white gazebo was embellished with wisteria vines and a cross to serve as the altar.

The attendance was slight since most invitees could not attend on such short notice. Christopher's family would never have been able to make the long trip from Arkansas in time for the ceremony, but many of his comrades were there to support their former classmate into this next phase of life. He promised his parents that he would send photographs of the wedding and of their new daughter-in-law, and he assured them that he had made the right choice. They would adore her, he wrote to them, and he and his new bride planned to start a family immediately.

Standing at the altar, they were a winsome couple, the perfect image of a new family starting their lives together: young, bold, exciting. Ellie wore her grandmother's gown regally, and her mother's eyes watered at the sight of her daughter in it. The headband on her veil was adorned with sprigs of baby's breath; the tulle hung thickly over her face and fell past her shoulders. She draped a bouquet of peace lilies over the long laced sleeves, letting them rest lightly on her arm. Her light-brown hair was lifted and pinned up and away from the high neckline of her dress.

Christopher's military uniform with polished shoes and brass buttons made him look like sovereignty as he walked beneath an elegant canopy of gleaming swords. His short black hair had been gelled and smoothed; his arched eyebrows framed his noble dark eyes. Their "I-dos" were clear and strong against the backdrop of breezes and birdsong and sniffles from some of the guests. After a kiss to solidify the union, a military brass band erupted in song and ushered the newlyweds to the veranda dance floor. Christopher held Ellie close to him, singing "Shoo Shoo Baby" in her ear as they swayed together. The band played the most popular hits for a couple of hours, and a few tipsy guests danced the jitterbug, interrupted only by Ellie's parents insisting that the guests needed to line up to send off the newlyweds. Rice was thrown amid the cheers as they ran to the getaway car that escorted them away from their old lives and into their new.

They stayed their first night as the Vaillant family at a bed and breakfast just north of town. All her life, she wondered and snickered and whispered with her girlfriends at slumber parties about what this night would be like. While all of her friends had different details, the verdict was all the same: It would be magical. It would be the induction and coronation of womanhood. It would be tender and romantic and meaningful, and it would be a bond that could never be broken between man and wife.

But she was wrong. Her friends were wrong. Instead, it was regrettable.

And that was the final flag.

There was no magic or tenderness or romance. He was callous. Demanding. *Do this. Now do that. You're my wife. I'm your captain. Do this again. Do that again.*

It hurt her. It repulsed her. It incensed her. She tried to refuse but he commanded otherwise. It was the worst night of her life.

The next morning Christopher was to be picked up by a military vehicle. A horn honked from the street curb. As he leaned down and kissed her, he told her that their house at Fort Bragg was ready and that her train ticket and some money for travel were on the dresser. He thanked her for an amazing wedding night.

"I have to go now, my bride. I'll be at Fort Moultrie getting briefed until tomorrow, then I ship out. I can't say where. I can't say for how long. But I hope you'll miss me. I'm so glad I made you my wife," he whispered in her ear. "I can't wait to get home to you again. Our home." He stroked her hair and leaned down to nuzzle her ear, then put his hand on her hip and gripped her forcibly. "I love you, Eleanor Vaillant. I'll be back soon. I'll write if I can."

She pretended to be sleeping until she heard his steps fading and the car door shut. Then she cringed and she cried.

She knew she had to do it. She had to go. The train to North Carolina left that afternoon, and she was supposed to be on it.

She could make a lot of things, she thought, as she picked her wedding dress up off the floor and crammed it into her valise. She could make dinner and breakfast. She could make the bed and make pies. She could make a deal and make acquaintances and make a fire in the hearth and make her own way in this war-weary world. But she could not make what the poets called love. You either love someone or you don't. You can want it to come; you can hope and pray with every breath that it will come, and sometimes, for the lucky and the few, it does come. But love cannot be manufactured. It cannot be created in laboratories nor forged in fire nor torn from the pages of Shakespeare. It either is or it isn't.

She would never be able to love him, she decided, so she would leave him. She couldn't run home; her parents would likely disown her. Her friends would think she had lost her mind, passing up such a handsome and respectable husband and a lifetime of being taken care of. Her sister would call her selfish and ignorant. Christopher would call her an ingrate.

She would have to disappear where no one could find her. She would have to get on that train and never show up in North Carolina. She'd check the itinerary when she got to the station and find a place to disembark. Somewhere no one would suspect. She would find a job in munitions or textiles or clerical work. It wasn't so unusual, she convinced herself, for women to work now. They needed women to fill the vacancies left by the soldiers sent to war. There would be plenty of opportunities for her to be self-sufficient and free. Truly free.

Ellie took a warm, fragrant bath to wash away the night and dressed in the smart outfit her mother had bought for her maiden voyage: a straight, fitted navy blue skirt that stopped just below the knee with a matching jacket that was cut short to hug her waistline. A white silk blouse and a navy beret tilted to the side made her outfit complete and gave her a sense of confidence that was unfamiliar to her. She left the bed unmade and plucked the train ticket and cash off the dresser, then made her way to the train that would take her north to her new life.

***

At the back of the train, Ellie twisted the wedding band on her finger nervously and watched the passing trees grow taller and the fallow fields wider. She tried to identify the scarce crops as they passed, but it was getting dark and it was raining and she dreamed again about her garden.

The train's next stop would be the last before Fort Bragg. If she was going to go through with this, if she was really going to do this, she would have to get off there. She rechecked the itinerary. Florence, South Carolina. She had never heard of Florence. It was as foreign to her as Florence, Italy, or Florence Nightingale. But Florence was the name of a woman, and women helped women. Florence would help her. Florence would hide her inside her hope chest of anonymity.

Her thoughts returned to her sordid wedding night, and she tugged at her wedding band. She pulled it off her finger and wanted to throw it out of the window into the pine trees that were passing slower and slower. Instead, she tucked it into the inside pocket of her purse and zipped it shut. Her hands were shaking, and she pulled out the little bit of cash that Christopher had left for her. She wouldn't need anything else. No identification that would link her present to her past. No keys to the house where she was supposed to start a family. No monogrammed handkerchief with her new initials that had been a wedding gift. No lipstick that Christopher insisted that she wear because it was his favorite. None of it. She would leave it all behind.

The train lurched and slowed, and Ellie could feel the rails scrubbing beneath her. She felt her stomach twist and drop, and self-doubt seized her tight as a mother's grip on her disobedient child's wrist. What if she really needed Christopher? What if she hadn't tried hard enough to be a good wife? She hadn't tried at all, actually. She had only been Mrs. Vaillant for one day and one horrible night. Maybe she wasn't being fair to him or her parents. Her parents had given her everything she needed to grow into a proper young woman. This would devastate them; they didn't deserve that. She was being selfish and childish.

She couldn't even remember the last time she had gone farther than a city block away from home by herself. They walked to church as a family. She accompanied her mother to the markets. Elisabeth walked with her to piano lessons. She had never even driven a car by herself. Did she really expect to step off this train into a world unknown and prosper? She was just a girl pretending to be a woman, a foolish, selfish girl who thought that putting a gold band around her finger would make her a woman.

The train screeched and squealed and finally came to a stop. A puff of steam and an audible exhale announced its arrival. The conductor came over the scratchy intercom, "Welcome to Florence, South Carolina. Passengers may now begin exiting the train."

Could she do this? She felt nauseous. Dizzy. Immobile. Like the weight of the Atlantic Ocean was on her. She looked at her purse in the seat beside her, and she stood.

Trembling, she stepped out into the cold rain.

Chapter Three

My feet are growing feeble now,
My legs are spent and sore.
I've trod on sticks and stones and sand,
O'er mountains—every shore.
I'm heading for the Promised Land
But first, I've one more task.
So carry me, Lord, carry me,
I've one more dream to cast.

The storm outside drew a deep breath and exhaled. The sleet tapped on the windows, keeping time with the rhythm of the train as it gathered speed. The wind pressed against the stiff tops of the pine trees, and the steel-gray clouds hung low and held the earth hostage.

The steady motion of the locomotive lulled the passengers into the comfort of their daydreams. The lights in the cars were dimmed, leaving only the warm glow of the electric sconces flickering with the occasional twitches of the train. The passengers had fantastic destinations awaiting them, and they were getting closer now with every blurry mile that raced beneath them. Each had an old home or a new home or a hopeful home calling to them—kind faces and anxious arms waiting to greet them. Everyone had something, even if it was only the siren call of the unknown: a new place with different streets and different smells and different faces.

Mary Lou Moore touched her fingertips to the window to feel the temperature outside. It was cold. Icy, even. She clasped her hands back in her lap to warm them. It seemed her hands were always cold these days, she thought. She moved her wedding band up and down against her arthritic knuckle. A young man in uniform sat across from her reading a newspaper. She couldn't see his face.

"Departing Florence, South Carolina," the conductor announced. "Next stop: Fayetteville, North Carolina."

"Young man," Mary Lou interrupted the soldier from his newspaper. He dropped it just below his eyes to see if the old woman was talking to him.

"What's your name?"

"Corporal Hendrix, ma'am." He was a little annoyed at the abrupt inception of conversation.

"Well good. What's your first name?"

"Harold."

"Harold, pleasure to meet you. You can call me Miss Mary Lou," she informed him.

"Thank you," he answered sarcastically and lifted his paper again to resume reading.

Mary Lou thought about the name Hendrix. There was a Hendrix family in the next town over—good people, except for the one sister that married some hobo and brought him home for the whole family to have to take care of—but other than that, she didn't know any Hendrixes. Sounded Dutch. Or maybe German. Neither could be trusted. He could be a spy hiding behind that American uniform, she considered. You never know these days. She would need to investigate further.

"Harold," she interrupted him again.

He dropped his paper. "Corporal," he corrected her.

"How do I know you're really a corporal, Harold?" she challenged.

"Because it says so right here." He pointed to the patches on his sleeve.

"Well this broach is a Queen Anne cameo inlay, but that doesn't make me Queen Anne now, does it?" She pointed to the cameo broach pinned to her pink cashmere sweater.

"I suppose not." He sounded annoyed by her counterargument.

"Are you German?"

"Sorry?"

"German. Your name sounds German."

"I'm not German, ma'am."

"Well what are you?"

"American."

"Don't you super sass me, young man. I know you have a mama, and I know she raised you better than to mouth off to your elders." Mary Lou re-situated her soft pink handbag in the seat beside her and pinched the top closed like an offended woman pins an open-necked blouse closed on her chest.

The corporal folded up his newspaper, an act of concession.

"Hendrix is Dutch," he said matter-of-factly. "My grandfather defected here in 1892. I've been serving in the army for seven years, and I have a birthmark on the backside of my left shoulder. I enjoy long balmy walks on the beach, and my favorite food is a Coney Island hot dog. Is there anything else you want to know?"

"Yes, there is. I want to know why your daddy didn't whip your tail with a wide leather belt when you were a youngin'. Then maybe you wouldn't have such a smart mouth. Does your mama know you act like this? Is she picking you up at the train station? Because if she is, I'm going to let her know that she has raised a mighty disrespectful young man."

Mary Lou lifted her chin and turned her face away from him. Her white hair was ear-length, carefully curled and set, and there was a faint impression on the crown of her head where her hat had been earlier. Behind her thick glasses were misty gray eyes framed by the deep lines and creases of a seventy-something-year-old woman. She had age spots on her cheekbones and more growing into her hairline, and the wrinkles etched into her forehead had not yet settled on her cheeks. The pink blush she had applied to the last smooth surface on her face was the same color as her sweater, as were her painted thin lips, and they were perched and ready to fire the next round of ammunition.

"Well, ma'am, that would be difficult since both of my parents have passed recently," the corporal told her. He lowered his eyes and waited.

"Well, I am very sorry about that." And she was. She reached over and patted the top of his hand. "I'm very sorry. That must be hard."

She leaned back and turned to the window even though she knew there was nothing to see but her own gossamer reflection. She pinched the top of her purse closed again and checked her broach to make sure it was secure.

"It's not an easy thing to lose people," she spoke without looking at the corporal. "And I reckon it's not supposed to be. But here we are, and we just have to take it, don't we. The Lord giveth and the Lord taketh away. But I swanty, sometimes He giveth and taketh away the wrong ones. You know what I mean? The wrong ones. And I'll tell you this, if I have to hear one more preacher tellin' me that it must've been the Lord's will, and that it's just a part of life, and that my husband is no longer in pain now and he's happy and dancin' in heaven, I'm gonna jerk a knot in him. Tellin' me like I don't already know. Of course he's in heaven. Lord never made a better man than my Milton. I mean it. Not a kinder, gentler man ever walked the face of this earth. And you think I don't already know he's not in pain anymore? You think I'm an ott? His heart's as healthy as a mule's now. But nobody will ever convince me that he's up there joyful and celebrating, not without me being there with him. I know he misses me. I just don't know why he left me. I know he didn't want to. I bet he pleaded with Peter at the gate to have more time with me. He wouldn't have wanted to leave me here alone. But the Lord took him against both of our wills, and I don't have any right to ask the Lord why. I know he's up there looking down at me, and I know he's sad about it. I can feel it. And I'm down here looking up at him, and I'm mighty sad too. So I tell myself every day, 'Mary Lou, just get through today. We'll tackle tomorrow tomorrow. Let's just get through today.'"

She unsnapped her purse and pulled out a handkerchief with pink stitching around the edges.

"And don't you know," she continued, "he would never argue with me? Sixty-three years of marriage, and he would not argue with me. I tried, but he would just stand there like a brick wall and let me have my tantrums. I'd be mad as fire, but no matter what, he'd still kiss me three times before he walked out of the door for work, three times when he got back home, and then before we went to sleep every night. Three times." She demonstrated in the air three quick kisses. "As soon as I see him again, I promise you he'll greet me with three kisses. I just know it." Her eyes watered again. "But I've got to see that great-grandbaby of ours first, Sugar Lump," she said up to the ceiling of the train. "I've got to squeeze our great-grandbaby first."

"I'm sorry about your husband, Miss Mary Lou," Harold said quietly.

"Thank you. Some people have told me that I talk too much, and I suppose I just did, so they may be right. But there's something about you, young man, that makes me feel like I need to know more about you. Tell me about your parents."

"There's not too much to tell. They were wonderful people taken too soon. Car accident. I don't mean to be rude, but I don't like talking about it."

"Well I suppose I can understand that. Are you married?"

"Yes, ma'am. Got two little girls. Maggie and Annie. They're twins."

"Well then, you have your hands fuller than a stocking on Christmas morning. I know they'll be excited to see their daddy. I suppose that's where you're going? Home?"

The corporal nodded and finally smiled.

"I'm headed to see a precious little darling myself. I got a new great-grandbaby." She pushed the tissue back into her purse and snapped it shut.

"Only four weeks old. His name is Toby." She considered this. "If you had a boy, would you name him 'Toby'?"

"Can't say that I would or wouldn't."

"Well I think it's ridiculous. What an awful name for a baby. I cannot for the life of me understand what possessed my son-in-law to name that baby Toby. Makes me think of toes. Stinky, dirty, smelly toes. Now why would you want to name your baby after stinky toes? Toby. Just say it out loud. Toby. Bless his heart, he's got to go through all his life sounding like a foot." She shook her head. "The only thing that would make it any worse is if they painted his nursery purple. Purple has got to be the saddest color on earth. It's just plain tacky. Makes my stomach hurt to look at it. Did you notice that this train is part purple?"

"No, I guess I didn't notice that."

"It's got a big fat purple stripe glommed all down the side of it. I almost turned around when I saw it at the station. Someone should have lost his job for that one. Who takes a beautiful piece of modern machinery and paints it purple? Does your wife like purple, Harold?"

"I suppose she does. I've never known anyone to not like purple, until now."

"Well, you do her and your girls a favor and don't ever dress them in purple. It's morbid. Depresses me just thinking about it. They'll look like a band of bruises walking around." She shook her head at the thought. "Well, Toby, or purple or not, I cannot wait to sink my fingers into those little fat rolls on his legs. I'm gonna squeeze the mischief out of him. Lord knows, there isn't anything purtier on God's green earth than fat rolls on a baby." She balled her fists in excitement.

***

Harold was beginning to find this old woman far more entertaining than the newspaper. He folded the paper neatly and laid it across his lap. She reminded him of his own grandmother. He remembered walking hand in hand with her down the tidy sidewalks of town to the dime store where she would treat him to whatever candy he picked out of the barrels that were almost as tall as him. His favorites were the Mary Janes and the maple candies. His grandmother would treat him to a root beer float, too, and they'd sit at the small table at the window looking out at the streets busy with shoppers, baby carriages, and cars driving slowly and braking for pedestrians. Everyone seemed so happy. He was happy. That was before Harold knew about war. That was before he knew men could be so cruel and so empty and so self-righteous to think that they should own one another. But now he knew. So he fastened the armor around his heart, and he polished his shield and vowed to spend the rest of his life fighting for those who are too downtrodden to fight for themselves. He despised the Nazis and everyone who fought for them. They wouldn't win. They couldn't win.

Unnaturally, Harold's grandmother outlived his parents. They were on the way home from a picture show last year when a car swerved into their lane at top speed, killing them instantly. The police officers said his parents were still holding hands when their bodies were pulled from the mangled car.

His grandmother mourned the tragedy by resolving to be the best great-grandparent to Harold's twins that anyone could ever dare to be. Despite her arthritis and other inevitable geriatric ailments, she made it a point to take Harold's twins anywhere she could manage. She recreated their walks to the dime store and spoiled their appetites. She took them to the park to feed the ducks the sandwich crusts they had been saving. She taught them to bake cookies and showed them how to lie in the grass and make shapes in the clouds that mirrored their billowing imaginations.

Harold dropped his head at the memory that was coming now. He didn't want it. He tried to look out of the train's window and blink it away, but it kept coming. It rushed into him with such a gust of force that he gripped his armrests for the impact. The circus. His grandmother wanted to take his twins girls to the circus. Harold's wife was thrilled, too, and she dressed the girls in their church dresses and put their hair in matching ribbons. Their white lace socks were turned down to the ankle, the black patent shoes were buckled and wiped clean, and the hem of their dresses matched the lacy trim on the socks. It would be an experience like none other. They would see real live elephants and tigers and glittering acrobats swing through the air on what seemed like a string, and there would be bands playing music and it would be spectacular. And it was. Their cheeks hurt from smiling and their hands were red from clapping.

Then the smell of smoke came. Was it from the cannons? Another dramatic performance beginning in the next ring? But then there were screams and people running and stampeding as the tent became a wall of fire. His wife grabbed the girls by their dresses and threw them on the ground to crawl out under the closest shred of canvas that wasn't in flames. She went back to get Harold's grandmother, but she couldn't be found in the mob, and then the tent collapsed under the weight of the fire. The wooden beams splintered into shards while flames dripped like lava and the smoke overwhelmed the imploding tomb. Harold's wife crawled to the last opening in the canvas and found their girls. They were sooty and shaken and terrified, but safe. They called for their grandmother, but the roar of the fire and the wailing sirens of the approaching fire trucks drowned their voices. Harold's grandmother never made it out.

Another loved one lost. When does it end?

Harold blinked quickly to regain his composure as Mary Lou's words came back to him, "Sometimes He giveth and taketh away the wrong ones."

He looked over at Mary Lou; her chin was dropped and her eyes were closed. She was snoring a little.

He checked his watch: 12:40 a.m. They would soon be in Fayetteville, and then he only had one more stop before he was home. Then he would be holding his wife and his girls at the same time, and he would temporarily forget about the war and his parents and his grandmother. He would be the master of his own fate, if just for a while, and he would try not to wonder why his family seemed stalked and plagued by tragedy. He would ignore the recurring question asked every year in his family of who would be next, and he'd put away the images of gunfire and planes dropping bombs and barbed wire fencing around trenches. He would be safe at home with his wife and his girls and pretend for their sakes and his that there was no such thing as premonition. There was no such thing as foreboding or intuition or something not feeling right.

He looked around the passenger car. Most passengers were sleeping. He saw a chaplain in the front with the Bible opened on his knee. He saw the young soldier sitting across from him, staring out into nothing. He saw the pregnant woman sleeping with her hand on her stomach, her face warm and her countenance content. Her husband sat beside her, clutching her other hand in his. He remembered that feeling. It was as true as love could get.

Dozens of other passengers slept, waiting for the morning when they would all be where they wanted to go. Harold wanted to sleep himself, but he couldn't close his eyes just yet. Something didn't feel right. Something felt very wrong.

Chapter Four

The train keeps roaring forward now,
It has no time to lose.
Closer, closer to the end
To slake the wanderer's Muse.
The Cyclops beam stabs through the night;
Its light finds sleet and snow.
The steel ties sway 'neath the journey's weight
And quiver down below.

The southbound Tamiami Champion, Atlantic Coast Line locomotive No. 91, heaved southward away from the double track depot in Fayetteville, North Carolina. The streetlamps hovering over the station were blurred by the sleet and snow of a rare southeastern winter storm. These conditions made many passengers late in boarding the train, and the engineer was frustrated by the delay. He ran a tight shift, and this would be a black mark on his nearly impeccable record. He pulled the timepiece from his pocket and noted 12:35 a.m. They would have to make up the time, he reasoned. It would be a simple enough task this time of night; there would be little need to slow down for traffic at the intersections, and no one would be out in this miserable weather. This train was Miami bound, and Miami would be a welcome sight from this swath of winter sludge and depression. The engineer let his mind flash to warm blue waters and white sand, and a martini for him and one for a beautiful woman. He inched the lever forward. Faster. Faster now, he coaxed.

"Rough night out there," the conductor said as he returned from gathering tickets. He pulled the collar up around his neck. "I tell ya, I grew up around these parts, and it isn't too often we get one of these. It sure is pretty, though."

The train shot its headlight beam into the freckled night air. Floating snowflakes were mixed with pelting sleet, and the sleet bounced off the steel ties of the dual tracks.

"What's the temperature read?" the engineer asked.

"Twelve degrees. Colder than your ex-girlfriend's stare," he joked.

"Not funny."

"How is ole Helen anyway? Hear from her much?"

"She comes around from time to time trying to reconcile. Says she'll change. Wants me to give her another shot."

"Well, why don't ya?"

"Because people never really change, you know. Not even if they want to, not even if they really believe they will. They just fake it long enough to get what they want, and then you have to start all over again trying to change them. That goes on awhile, and then you figure you've been together too long to just give up, so you just keep putting up with it. And on and on. I'm done with that. The trick is to find someone you never want to change in the first place. I aim to find her in Miami."

"Well good luck with that," the conductor chuckled and pulled out a book from his bag.

"What's that?"

"Hemingway. *For Whom the Bell Tolls*."

"Isn't that about war? Why in the hell would you want to read a book about war? Haven't you had enough of it? I have. I'm sick of it all."

"It isn't about this war. It's the Spanish war, I think. I haven't started it yet. Figured you'd get this bird slidin' along these rails and I could relax and kill a little time. Besides, it'll help me stay awake tonight."

The engineer seemed to remember something and cleared his throat. "Ask not for whom the bell tolls, it tolls for thee."

The conductor pulled off his hat and hung it on a gear knob. He opened the cover of the book and turned straight to the first chapter and read the same lines the engineer had just recited. "How'd you know about that?"

"It's an old poem by John Donne, a Brit. My grandfather used to recite it to me. I never really understood it until I grew up and read it for myself. But my grandfather thought it was the finest thing ever put on paper. Anyway, that's the title of your book there, right?"

"Yeah. I don't know about all that, I just like Hemingway. He isn't afraid to tell you that things don't always end well."

The train approached a road crossing and the engineer reached up to pull the rope to sound the whistle. It was an eerie sound during the nighttime, and especially during storms. The clouds, the mist, and the darkness carried the sound farther and slower than it did during the day. It echoed deep and long and wide without the daylight there to curb it. The wail was mournful, and it wandered through the pine trees, seeping into the farmers' soil on the Carolina countryside, searching for something and sometimes finding it, sometimes not. If the agony of loneliness could be made into a sound, it would be the whistle of a train in the dark.

The engineer pulled his clipboard off the hook and checked his charts.

"Approaching Rennert," he announced.

"No boarding there tonight, sir," the conductor confirmed.

"Good. One less thing to slow us down so we can get to Miami."

The conductor returned to his reading while the engineer recorded the time and date: 12:45 a.m., Thursday, December 16, 1943. He slowed the train as the hazy lights of Rennert grew into view and gave a few short whistles to any of the station attendees that may be working. They barreled through the small, one-intersection town, all eighteen cars slinking single file in their monotonous rhythm.

Rennert's streetlamps were gone in only a few seconds, and the engineer nudged the lever back up toward top speed.

"So you're from these parts, eh? What made you leave?"

"Too many hills and rows."

"Hills? I don't see any hills around here."

"Tobacco hills. That's just what we called the rows in the fields."

"No fun, huh?"

"Not a bit. Well," he thought aloud, "I suppose some of it was all right. But I wasn't cut out for it. And I sure as heck didn't want to do that for the rest of my life. As soon as I turned sixteen, I bought myself an old car off a neighbor, drove north, and got the heck out of this heat. You ain't never felt heat like the heat in a Carolina tobacco field in August. You ever put in tobacco?" he asked the engineer.

"Nope. My pops ran an auto shop in Trenton. I got my hands soiled aplenty, but from grease, not dirt."

"Sometimes I liked it. It just got into you somehow. What is it they say? 'The dirt is in your blood if your blood is in the dirt.' Something like that. But it's true. If you own the land, and you got your blood, sweat, and tears in it, and you make things grow on it, it feels good. It's hard, and sometimes you wonder why you bother with it, but it just feels like that's the way it's supposed to be or something. We'd set out the crack of dawn trying to beat the heat, but before lunchtime the monkey'd be on my back and I'd have to set down and take a breather. The worst was cropping sandlugs. I hated that job. After a hard thunderstorm the bottom leaves, we called 'em sandlugs, were beaten down into the dirt, and I'd pull those buggers out and hold the leaves between my arm and my side as I went so I could pull 'em quicker. By the end of a few rows there'd be so much gum on me that my arm would plum stick to my body. My old man kept a bar of lye down by the pond just for that, so I'd have to jump in the pond and scrub down with the lye. I don't know which was worse, the gum or the lye. Suckerin' was tough too. Had to reach way up and pop those flowers off 'cause they sucked the life right outta the rest of the plant, and that goo would slam run down your arm and gum up in your armpit hairs. Back to the pond I'd go. The lye'd scrub the flesh right off your body, but it never could get your fingernails clean. I spent months with my hands jammed in my pockets when I was in town so the girls wouldn't think I was so filthy."

He stared out of the window with a grin on his bristled face. "Tobacco money was good, though. Come auction day, everyone, and I mean everyone, was in a good mood. Our farm had some of the best quality leaves in the state, and we knew it. A golden leaf was a golden ticket. Plus, my daddy had a farmhand who was left-handed, and so when he graded and tied the leaves together, it made for a knot that lay a little different and caught the attention of the buyers. We never left a warehouse with a single leaf left. One time some slimeball stole a pallet of our tobacco, and the only way the cops were able to identify it was by that left-handed tie."

Maybe he did miss it. Maybe it would have been a good life. He missed the camaraderie among the farmhands, the chicken bogs at the end of the season, the end of the day's hot meal and sweet tea and then sleeping the best sleep he's ever slept. Maybe he did miss going to town the day of the sale and feeling the energy that was palpable in the autumn air. It was when hard work finally turned into something you could touch.

Farmers stood in tight circles and lit their cigarettes. "Best flue-cured in the whole country," they'd crow, and the other men would nod their heads and agree. "Them cotton boys think they got the cream, but tobacco's king, I tell ya. Tobacco's king." They'd nod their heads, "Yes, sir, it is. Tobacco's king."

Seeing the sleet hit the tracks ahead of him and the snow spiraling in the air made the conductor remember, too, that the farmer is unendingly at the mercy, or lack thereof, of nature. At least trains were consistent, he justified his choice. At least they can work through all kinds of weather, and the paychecks still keep coming. He didn't have to look to the skies or the ways the birds flew or the color of a leaf to determine his fate, he just had to look at the schedule.

The worst of all the weather on the tobacco farm was hail. Many afternoons his father sat and tapped his blackened fingernails on the kitchen table, looking out of the window toward the gathering purple skies as the afternoon thunderstorms piled up on the horizon. The heavy air almost sizzled with electricity, and the thunder echoed low. Was there hail in those clouds? When the clouds moved in closer, he'd step out on the porch and light a cigarette and watch the birds.

"You ever seen a bird die in a hailstorm?" he asked his son. "Me neither. They aren't stupid. So when the birds aren't flying before that first breeze whips 'em, they've taken shelter. Mockingbirds are 'bout the smartest. You watch them for a while, and you'll learn everything you need to know about livin'." That year his father learned that buyers wouldn't buy leaves with holes in them.

Suddenly the train jolted and jerked him back from his memory. The engineer instantly reached for the brake lever and yanked it back with all of his weight. The conductor was launched to the floor, and his book flew from his lap and smacked against the wall. Beneath them, the train shook violently, and a piercing screech pealed out as the wheels seized up and ground against the steel rails. Blinding sparks shot out in torrents into the dark until the train came to a stop. Steam and smoke hissed out from the underbelly like a legion of sinewy serpents, and the crew hurried and jumped out of the cars with their shaky lanterns and panic-stricken faces.

The conductor scrambled to the door and leaped out of the train and bellowed his orders, his arms frantic and pointing, "Check for fire! Check the passengers! Every car!"

The crew crawled on their hands and knees, holding lanterns up under the belly to find her plight. Their thick, wide pant legs and heavy boots made agility difficult, and they slipped repeatedly on the icy rail ties. The mammoth iron wheels of the locomotive were hot through their gloves as they tried to investigate.

"Got something leaking under here, boss," one man shouted, half of his body underneath the second car. "She's broke right here! She's cracked all right. Brake pipe gone too. That's why she froze up on us."

Another man was already on the way to find the torches and repair tools when a voice yelled in the distance.

"We lost some! We lost some!" He couldn't reach his crew fast enough before he yelled again. "Last three cars are gone! I don't see them anywhere!" He couldn't catch his breath, and the terror in his voice materialized into the vapor pouring out of his mouth and nostrils.

The winter air pricked the backs of their necks, but the circumstance chilled them more. The conductor ordered the crew to run the tracks and tree line for the missing cars, and not to stop until they found them. Then he called for the fireman, "Get the fuses and light them a ways up the track! There's another train coming northbound tonight on the other track, and we need to let him know to slow down. Go! Go!"

The fireman disappeared into a car and fumbled through the red metal emergency box mounted on the wall. He quickly reemerged holding a light and a safety fuse, a large-headed match capable of staying lit in strong wind. The fireman and his crew knew the protocol well and had practiced these scenarios many times before. His training taught him that he was to position himself well ahead of the stalled train, place the fuse flare on the tracks and light it, then wave a lantern at the oncoming train to signal that there is danger ahead. So the fireman gripped his supplies and started running to take his position ahead of the southbound locomotive. The bitter cold air bit at his ears and the sleet stung his eyes, making each hurried step no better than a blind guess. The fireman slipped and lost his footing several times, trying to negotiate the icy rail ties in the dark. The shouts of his crewmates and the hammering and sparks of their tools grew muffled with the distance, and soon all he could hear was the crunch of his feet finding gravel between the ties. He slowed to a trot to gauge his distance. *Just a little farther*, he thought. The pine trees blew above him, and the icy needles clicked against each other like witches' nails and then fell and shattered on the ground around him. *Just a few more steps*, he told himself. But with his next step, his boots shot out from under him. He instinctively threw his arms down in front of him to brace the fall, dropping both the fuse and the light onto the sodden tracks. The fireman crashed down on top of the beacon, its glass and bulb shattering into a hundred horrible pieces. The light was gone. The fuse was wet and mangled and could not be lit.

The conductor ran to the rear of the train, recounting the cars in hopes that the men had just miscounted amid the chaos, but they were indeed three cars short. He saw lantern lights bobbing back and forth in the distance, and by the howls and shouting, he judged that the cars had been found. Frantically, he ran toward them. *Please don't let anyone be hurt*, he thought. *Please don't let them be hurt.*

Three cars had derailed from the rear of the train. "Busted rail, boss," one man explained, pointing to the broken rail. "Coupling broke and they jumped the track. Nobody hurt too bad though, boss. Just some scrapes and bruises. We're getting everybody off the train now."

The train cars had fallen sideways, blocking the parallel northbound track. The passengers were crawling out of the doors, carrying whatever belongings they had on the seats beside them. They were in shock and moved in silent lines off the rails to the shelter of the tree line. A crewman was guiding them with his lantern and trying to keep them calm.

"That's right," he coaxed them. "Everything is going to be fine. Right over here, ma'am. We're gonna get you comfortable, and we'll have this train going again in no time."

"Where are we supposed to go?" A stunned woman was holding on to the elbow of a soldier.

"Just to that line of trees there, ma'am, until we can secure the other cars." He pointed them in the direction of the embankment away from the tracks. "Not to worry, now. There's nothing to worry about. Anyone hurt?"

"But where's the rest of the train?" The woman continued. "What happened to it?"

"The rest of the train is about a half mile up the track. We got derailed back here, and the train is stopped and making some repairs," the conductor answered her.

A mother filed out of a car, clutching her baby against her chest and trying to soothe him. She had the blanket wrapped around him so that only his nose was visible. "He can't be out here! It's freezing! He'll freeze to death! Why can't we get onto the other part of the train?"

"Yes, ma'am, I know it's cold. We're going to get a fire going here as soon as everyone is safely evacuated. They're repairing the damage to the front cars as fast as they can, and when they give us the signal that everything is safe, we'll get everybody back onboard. Right now we need to get everyone together and get you warm. Hey, Johnny," the conductor yelled back to his crewmen. "Grab all the blankets you can find in there! We need to keep these people warm! Pillows and newspapers, anything. Everything's wet out here!" He tried to speak to each passenger as they passed in an effort to keep them calm and orderly.

"Yes, sir, this way, and thank you for your service," he addressed several soldiers. "I know you'll be glad to get home, and we're gonna get you there real soon. Anyone hurt? Yes, sir, it is very cold out here. We'll get you warmed up. Right over here please."

The passengers followed the directions like stunned and mum sheep and only began assessing themselves once they sat in huddled circles and the fires were lit and they could see one another's faces. Some had gashes on their heads, the blood slowly dripping down their faces, and others were beginning to feel bone-heavy pains in their arms and legs. *Just bruised*, they decided. *Just a few stitches, and no lives lost.* They couldn't believe their simultaneous good and bad fortune, and they comforted each other by speaking of home. *We'll get there soon enough*, they reminded themselves. *At least we're alive and we'll get to see our families for Christmas*, they said with relief.

A younger man wearing a woolen Harvard jacket pulled a Bible from inside his coat pocket and went from group to group, putting his free hand on shivering shoulders and speaking softly and saying prayers of thanks. "Let's bow for a word of prayer. Lord, God, we thank You for this night and we thank You for putting Your hedge of protection around us. Please help us to feel Your peace among us, Lord, and keep us safe and strong during this frightening time, Lord."

It could have been so much worse, they consoled themselves.

The pastor then remembered that the Bible his great-grandfather had given him was still on the train. Its pages were well worn and disintegrating, but the pastor kept it with him in a small tin box as a reminder. "Know who you are and where you're going," his great-grandfather always told him. He had to go back in to get it.

"Pastor, sir," a crewman stopped him. "You can't go back in there."

"I'll only be a second. I left something very, very important in there. I know exactly where it is. It'll only take me a second." He walked quickly to the cars, ignoring the crewman's instructions, and slipped on the ice while trying to hoist himself back in the door. He had not accounted for the darkness inside and fumbled around blindly searching for the tin box.

The crewmen gathered to discuss how to get the cars off the parallel rails while the passengers gathered beneath the pines and looked at the disabled train in disbelief. It was almost 1:30 a.m., and the waning snow drifted sporadically like ashes through the frozen air. The crew wrapped the plaid Pullman blankets around the women and the elderly and stoked the fires with anything they could find. Several soldiers began snapping dead pine branches from the trees for more kindling, and others offered their coats and confident statures to help quell the passengers' flaring fears. *Help will be here soon*, they stated. *It won't be too much longer*, they hoped.

***

The fireman was on his hands and knees, frantically trying to find the busted fuse. He snatched his thick gloves off so he could feel for the scattered pieces in the dark. Shattered glass sliced through his hands, but he couldn't feel the blood. He thought he heard a rumbling in the distance. The track beneath him started to vibrate ... stronger ... then stronger. A train was coming. Their sister train, the Tamiami Champion No. 8, was barreling north on the dual tracks at full speed. They wouldn't have had time yet to receive notification about the disabled cars in their path. They had to be warned, but the fuse was shattered. The light was shattered. The only light was the Cyclops beam that stabbed at the dark night, motionless and helpless and portentous and only minutes away from a hell that few had known.

The fireman jumped up and ran back toward his crew. Tears and terror streamed from his eyes.

"Train!" he screamed. "Train!"

It was the only word he could think of to shout, and like the nightmare he had so often as a child, help was near, but his voice was never loud enough to reach them. He turned back to the oncoming train and screamed hysterically and waved his arms, but the night was too dark, and the air was too cold, and the only thing he heard was his own breathing and his heart despairing and his numb feet pounding.

"Train!" he shrieked again, falling to his knees. "Train!"

Chapter Five

I'm almost there,
I'm almost home!
I'm pealing 'round the bend!
I'll hold you, kiss you, worship you,
And never leave again.
Her wheels are churning faster now,
Her diesel curls in plumes.
Soon, my love, you will not need
Your cradle in this womb.

The dimly lit brass sconces flickered against the wallpapered walls of the Pullman car, glitching bright and then dull again with the swaying speed of the northbound train. The burgundy-and-crème damask pattern on the wallpaper was an effort at elegance and warmth, unnoticed now by those weary passengers that willfully succumbed to their somnolence. Their seats were reclined and the complimentary blankets pulled up to their chins to stave off the cold air that insisted on seeping through the panes in the glass windows. Heads rocked gently back and forth to the cadence of the wheels as most of the passengers were sleeping, dreaming of homecomings and lit Christmas trees and table-clothed tables lined with shining silverware and steaming dishes.

The yellow light lay like honey across the tops of the seats and those sitting there, ethereal and angelic as it framed the different wisps of hair like halos.

Mary Lou Moore slept with her pink purse shut and clutched in her lap, her fingers clasped together and resting on top of it. Her age spots were less visible now in the dimness, but the veins across her hands rose like ghosts across her knuckles and across the backs of her slender hands. Her wedding ring hung loose with the memory of time but refused to let go, and her small frame moved in accordance with the train. Her head rested just below the headrest, and with her mouth parted slightly, she snored.

Harold had been watching Mary Lou fade into sleep, needing to know she was comfortable and content before he would allow himself to drift off. He thought of her great-grandson with the name Toby, and he chuckled to himself. He thought of her deceased husband whom she still simultaneously celebrated and mourned, and he hoped that his wife would feel the same way about him when it was his time to pass. Funny, he noticed, how the only person capable of disarming him—other than his beautiful wife and twins—was a candid old woman on a train.

The burden of dying was a very real possibility to him, and until this war was over, it would be a possibility he awoke to every day. It's quite something, he thought, to open your eyes and wake up each day to the thought of dying, to the very real possibility of it. Seems like it would make one more ambitious, more motivated to achieve something wonderful. But it doesn't. At first, it just makes you scared. Makes you not want to climb out of bed in the morning. But after time, fear carves you down to dullness, and it just sits there, like an old friend on a long, meandering car ride who you don't feel obligated to speak to. He opened his heavy eyes again to check on Mary Lou. He heard her snoring lightly and wondered if she was dreaming of Milton.

He thought of his grandmother and if maybe she was watching over him. He didn't know about that stuff. He wasn't sure if he believed that the deceased can watch over the living, but he had to admit to the frequency with which he saw his grandmother's favorite flower. He saw gardenias in the most unlikely of places. When his troop landed on the beachhead in Salerno and the tanks plowed down the ramps off the boats onto the beach, shells fell around them and sprayed sand into the air in unpredictable, violent bursts. The sand fell like rain on his helmet. There were cacophonous shouts and orders and the sharp pops of gunfire, and as he crawled on his stomach through the dunes, he swore he saw a gardenia bush tucked into the trampled sea oats. He knew gardenias couldn't survive there, but he also knew what he saw, and somehow he survived the dunes that day too.

When his feet finally touched American soil, he saw a gardenia bush landside of the disembarkation ramp. He stopped in his tracks to confirm it by touching the velvety white blossom, and he picked a single petal and held it to his nose. When he boarded the Tamiami Champion in Jacksonville, a gardenia bush in a row of other bushes was the only bush in bloom. But maybe these were all just coincidences, and maybe he only noticed gardenias now because he was looking for them, looking for a reminder. Maybe he didn't really believe it that it was his grandmother watching over him. Maybe.

**

In the back of the train car, a serviceman eyed a pocketbook perched in a vacant seat. He was tempted to look inside of it, not to steal anything, but to identify it and return it to its rightful owner. He had been waiting for hours and many miles for someone to claim it, thinking that perhaps the owner had simply gone to the dining car or to the restroom. But no one ever came back for it. He knew it was of the utmost disrespect to look into a woman's personal belongings, but how else would he know to whom it belonged? Perhaps if he found an address inside, he rationalized, he could mail it back to the lady in case she had mistakenly left it behind. Now that everyone was asleep, he would look inside. No one would see him. He reached over the aisle silently and pulled the pocketbook into the empty seat beside him. It was a shiny white patent leather and had scalloped magnolias embroidered on the side. He unzipped it slowly so it wouldn't make a sound and pulled the contents out one by one. An unused handkerchief was on top. It was still folded and had the initials EMV in gold cursive letters sewn into the bottom corner. He pulled out a metal tube, lipstick, he assumed, and positioned it on the seat so it wouldn't roll off with the movement of the train. There were white gloves, also embroidered with magnolias, and a round compartment of some sort. He unsnapped it out of curiosity and opened it to find only a mirror inside. In a separate pocket he found a key. The key ring had an address tagged to it: 315 Dogwood Lane, Fort Bragg, North Carolina.

The man noticed the conductor coming toward him down the aisle, and he quickly shoved the items back into the purse and returned it to its original seat. The conductor looked back and forth at each row of passengers, stepping quietly as he patrolled to see that everyone was comfortable. When he reached the back of the car, he noticed the pocketbook and looked around to see if it belonged to someone nearby.

"Sir," the man addressed the conductor. "That pocketbook has been sitting there since around Florence, I believe. No one has claimed it."

"Gosh, I hope it isn't lonely," the conductor chuckled at his own joke. The man didn't laugh.

"Perhaps you could find an address in it? Mail it back to the owner?"

"Yes," the conductor used his serious tone now. "We'll hold this up front in case someone comes looking for it. If no one claims it by the end of the line, we'll turn it over to the authorities and let them decide how to handle it. You won't catch me digging through a woman's personal belongings," he chuckled again in spite of himself. "You'd have to be either a fool or a thief or both to go rummaging around in a lady's things." He reached over and tucked the pocketbook under his arm.

"Right. Just saying, it isn't too often that a woman leaves a purse unattended for so long," the man replied. He leaned his head back and closed his eyes to sleep.

**

In the front of the car, James Merritt kicked and jerked himself awake. Startled, sweat ran down his temple and cheeks and dripped from his jaw. He looked around for something to wipe his face with. The young chaplain offered his handkerchief.

James took it reluctantly. "Thanks."

"Nightmare?"

"Guess so." He didn't want to talk about it.

"I imagine after what you've been through, you have lots of nightmares."

"What do you know about what I've been through?" James snapped at the stranger's assumption and wiped the back of his neck.

"Your medal. You've got the mark of a hero, friend, and heroes don't become heroes without a little hell."

James glanced at the Bible sitting beside the chaplain on the bolted-down table.

"Oh, I forgot. I'm not supposed to say 'hell' now that I'm a chaplain," he said. He put his hand up to his brow. "But I still slip up sometimes. Forgive me. I'm Edwards." He extended his hand to shake.

"James." He half-heartedly shook the chaplain's hand. "No problem. I say 'hell' all the time. Hell, I live it." He didn't smile.

"Who's Luther?"

James flashed his dark eyes at Edwards.

"A comrade?" the preacher pushed to crack the door open. "You said his name a lot while you were sleeping. If you can call that sleeping."

"Listen. No disrespect. But I don't usually engage in conversations with strangers, especially about personal things. So I'd appreciate it if you'd quit asking me questions about things you don't know about. I'm just trying to get home, pal, and I don't need your help getting there."

"Understood." The preacher grabbed his Bible and pulled it to his knee. He opened it and tried to read, but the lights were too dim to see the tiny print.

"I've never been a soldier," he continued talking. "I can't imagine. I just fight for the Lord, and that's scary enough. I don't have to deal with being shot at or having bombs dropped around me or being oceans away from home. You have my respect."

The word caught James in the chest. He hadn't heard that word in a long time. *Respect*. He especially hadn't heard it about himself in a long time, if ever. The word was a warm blanket, and he didn't deserve to have it wrapped around his shoulders, so he threw it to the floor.

"I don't need your respect."

"Suit yourself, but you have it all the same."

Edwards didn't make eye contact with James but pretended to thumb through the pages of his Bible. A few moments passed, and the preacher assumed James was no longer directing his attention at him, so he closed his eyes and his mouth moved slightly in silent prayer.

James cringed at the possibility of those whispered words, knowing that they were for him. He wondered what the preacher was thinking about him. Surely nothing good.

Edwards opened his eyes and pulled a red-and-white pack out of his shirt pocket and extended a stick. "Cigarette?"

James accepted while Edwards searched for the matches in the same pocket. "I've started to think about quitting these things," he said matter-of-factly. He dangled the cigarette from his lips and lit a match. "Scientists are starting to suspect that tobacco's not so great for you. They say it turns your lungs black, or something like that. But so do coal mines. If you ask me, which you didn't, they don't have enough evidence to convince me yet, so I don't think I'm going to quit right now." He aimed the irony at James's eyes.

"The body's the temple, right?" James felt obligated to reply as the chaplain lit the match and brought it to the end of James's cigarette.

"I suppose. I drink, too, if you were wondering."

"You swear, smoke, and drink. Not a very good preacher, are you?" James blew a ring and watched it waft away.

"Probably not. I'm not exactly sure what does make a good preacher, though. Saying what people want to hear, or saying what they don't want to hear? Either way, I'm cuffed. You can't make everyone happy, so I just try to make Him happy."

"So you think it makes God happy that you cuss and carry on like the rest of us heathens?"

"I don't think He minds as long as I follow the rules."

"Ah, yes. Rules. Always rules."

"There's really only ten of them, you know."

"I've heard."

"So far, I've only broken eight of them. Let's see, I stole a butterscotch from the candy barrel when I was ten. I was jealous of my neighbor's house, and that was just last week. Seven bedrooms and a swimming pool. Can you imagine that? They have a swimming pool in their own backyard. They can swim whenever they want to. Just walk right out of their back door and sploosh! Swimming pool." He made a swimming motion with his hands. "What else. I have most certainly not always honored my father and my mother. I have skipped church, a lot, so I think that's probably the same as not honoring the Sabbath. I cried like a baby when my Steelers and those demonic Eagles had to merge this season. *Steagles.* Have you ever heard anything so ridiculous? Anyway, mourned it for days. Wouldn't step outside. I was so mad that I didn't so much as look up at the sky for a week. I wanted Elbie Shultz to run 'em all into the ground. I suppose being that upset about something as silly as that qualifies as idolatry. We've already covered that I cuss, and I have been known to lie on occasion. But, on a positive note, I have never cheated on a woman, and I haven't murdered anyone yet."

"What in the hell made you want to be a preacher with a record like that?" James shook his head and grinned for the first time in years. His teeth were clean and white, but one front tooth slightly overlapped the other.

Edwards considered the question. "Well, without sounding like a pamphlet nailed to a corner post, it's because I know I'm forgiven. You can't find true forgiveness anywhere else. Trust me, I've tried."

"That's cheap. So you can just go around breaking all the rules and doing what you want to, and all you have to do is say you're sorry and you get away with it in the end, huh? No wonder everybody hangs on to religion."

"Well, that's not quite the way it works. You can't break the rules intentionally or unintentionally, and you never really get away with anything. There are always consequences. You're either hurting yourself or hurting someone else. When I stole candy, I thought, 'It's just one piece.' But it hurt my mother. She was embarrassed and thought she had raised me better. I hurt Mr. Webber, the store owner. Some of my friends weren't allowed to play with me for a while. And I hurt myself because from then on no one could trust me. Who knew one little piece of candy could last so long? And they all forgave me, sure, after I apologized and promised to never do it again. But they didn't forget. Once the trust is gone, it doesn't ever come back. Not truly."

James thought of Luther's theory on forgiveness, and for a quick second, he thought he saw a flash of Luther in Edwards's eyes. He shook the image away.

"My father was an abusive alcoholic," the chaplain continued. He turned his gaze toward the window. The sleet streaked and jerked along the glass.

James was uncomfortable and wasn't sure what to do with all of this. He awkwardly smoothed down the hair on his head and shifted in his seat.

"I don't know why I'm telling you this. Maybe I just needed to get it off my chest. I've never told anyone that before. I even kept it a secret in seminary. It's an embarrassing thing to admit."

"Well that's some tough luck, for sure, but let's cut this short for both our sakes. I know what you're trying to do, but I'm not your friend and I'm not looking for a friend. I don't want to hear your sad stories so you can try to get me to open up and talk about myself and ask for forgiveness and be saved. I don't need any of that. I just want to be left alone and I just want to ride this train in peace until I can get home. Got it?" James jammed his fingers into his dark hair and pushed it back again. His hair was still damp with sweat.

Edwards considered this. "I tell you what. You tell me who Luther is, and I'll zip my trap shut for the rest of the trip. Deal?"

"Why do you want to know so bad? What's it to you who Luther was?"

"It was the way you said his name. Sounded important."

James was exasperated. "All right, fine. He was a guy in my platoon. Got shot. I couldn't do anything to help him and he died. That's who he was. That's it. Now, you hold up your end of the deal."

The chaplain nodded and gripped his Bible tighter.

James heard Luther's words again. *Forgiveness, my boys, is a beautiful thing.* He remembered the surprised look on Luther's face when he was shot, and then he remembered that he scrambled like a coward to his own safety and left his friend dying, bleeding to death in a makeshift hut in the mud and rain and so far away from home and so far from everything that he loved and lived for. Of all the men that didn't deserve that, Luther shouldn't have died that way. The next morning when he crawled back to the hovel and found his comrades bloody and prostrate, he checked their pulses and lifted Luther's eyelids just to be sure. He remembered the peace he saw in Luther's eyes, peace that had no business being in the presence of a man whose last breath was taken in agony. A lake after a storm, he thought. That's what Luther's eyes were like. *Forgiveness, my boys, is a beautiful thing.*

"I ran," James choked out a whisper. He looked out past the window and past the snow and ice that thickened with each northbound mile, and the words fled from him like prisoners racing for a gap in the barbwire fence. "I ran from the tent when they shot Luther and then they shot Michael, and I hid until I knew it was safe. I ran from home and I ran from church and from my father's rules and my mother's loyalty and I ran from my best friend because I might as well have killed him too. I ran from Meredith and I ran from my very own child. My own child! Who does that? Only monsters do that."

James put his head in his hands and doubled over; the tears on his face soaked into his pants at the knees. His shoulders heaved and shook silently, and he couldn't open his eyes—didn't want to. For the first time in his life, the tears and the guilt spilled from him in inconsolable torrents until there was nothing left in him. The chaplain placed the handkerchief on his knee, not wanting to break his promise to no longer speak to this broken man. James wiped his eyes on his sleeves and grabbed the handkerchief to wipe his nose. He didn't want to sit up and face the chaplain, but what did it matter now? His pride had been left on the tracks miles ago.

"I'm sorry," James finally said. He smoothed his hair and took a deep breath as he sat upright. "I didn't mean to let that happen. I shouldn't have cried like that."

"Sounds like you didn't have a choice; it was coming out sooner or later. Well, look, now here I've gone and broken another promise. I think you may be right, I'm not very good at this preacher thing." Edwards extended another cigarette, and James accepted.

"But doesn't it make you mad that men aren't supposed to cry?" Edwards asked. "If you think about it, as soon as we're born, we're taught not to cry. Babies cry, and the first thing mothers do is try like hell to get the baby to stop crying. They rock 'em, hold 'em, sing to 'em, stick bottles and pacifiers in their mouths, walk 'em, all just to get them to stop crying. Then when they're a little older, they fall down and scrape a knee at the park and the first thing a boy hears is, 'Stop crying. Toughen up. It's not that bad.' Older still and get a broken heart, and you're a wuss if your friends see you cry, let alone your father. Men aren't allowed to cry. Supposed to be strong. The rock of the family. But it makes me angry. We should be allowed to cry without being ashamed of it. I cry all the time. Not just when I'm sad, but I cry when I see something beautiful. Like a river running over rocks. Or when I hear something powerful, like a marching band in a parade or the national anthem. I cry like a baby at every ballgame, or like when the Steagles took the field the first time. But that was a cry of misery," he laughed quietly. "And I cry when I think about God too hard."

"Isn't it your job to think about God?"

"I guess. Can't explain it. Something comes over me sometimes, and I just want to cry because it feels good. Warm. Rich. So anyway, it's done."

James was too exhausted to fight and lifted his eyes to meet Edwards's gaze.

"What's done?"

"The things you said you did."

"I know. I'm the one that did them, remember?" He wasn't in the mood for games.

"So then that means you're forgiven."

"No, it doesn't."

"Sure it does."

"Listen, I haven't asked anyone for forgiveness, and I'm not going to. I did what I did, and I don't want to be pitied for it. I'll take what I deserve like a man, or like the man I haven't been."

"Forgiveness isn't pity. It's grace. There's a difference. And you have asked for it; you just did. You know you did wrong, you admitted doing wrong, and you're remorseful about it. It's the same as asking for it, just with a different succession of sentences. Just different words. So it's done. Finished. You're forgiven."

"My parents and Ben and Meredith will probably never forgive me. My kid, if I have one, and who I have never laid eyes on, won't forgive me. And God can't forgive me when I never asked for it. You're a fool, and you really are a lousy preacher." He could feel the water welling in his eyes again and he willed it away. No more crying.

"Maybe so." The chaplain ran his finger along the edges of the cover of his Bible. It was burgundy and leather bound and his name was printed in the bottom right corner in gold letters. He traced the letters slowly.

James knew he had hurt him. *Imagine that*, he thought. He had hurt someone again. He listened to the sounds of the train, steel gliding along steel, the long moan of the occasional whistle, the consistent growl of machination in progress. He imagined the sound it would make when it came into contact with his flesh. He pictured himself stepping out, chest and shoulders broad and standing face-to-face with the giant. Only this time he wouldn't be a coward. Would he feel anything? He hoped so. He hoped that he would feel the amalgamation of all the pain that he had caused everyone else in one colossal blow. Then it would be done. Then it would be finished—forgiven or not didn't matter.

***

Suddenly, the train lurched, and the brakes shrilled, and terror seized the passengers. There was no time for a gasp or a scream or a prayer.
Then, all was black.

Chapter Six

The whistle called, its mournful voice
A banshee in the night.
It cried for gods, for ghosts, for both
To banish Moirai's plight.
The only answer was the sound
Of darkness falling black;
The angels bowed their heads and pinned
Their wings behind their backs.

Pecan Locklear was awake. He sat at his kitchen table, listening to the sleet clicking against the tin roof like tiny fingernails tapping to come in from the cold. He remembered there was now a gash up there that he'd need to mend as soon as the weather broke. A pecan tree branch had fallen on the roof like a can opener earlier in the evening, unaccustomed to the unusual weight of ice and snow. The tree surely needed trimming, but he was hoping to wait until the spring before he had to scale the fat trunk with his handsaw. His father, Manny, had fallen that way, trimming the same tree. He reached too far and the rope didn't hold. Manny tried to land like a cat, but the fall broke his leg, or that's what his father figured. It wasn't a bad enough injury to see a doctor, he had told them. But truth be told, there wasn't enough money to see the doctor. So the bones in Manny's broken leg grew back as crooked as a sea oak.

"Guessing," Manny always insisted. "That's all doctors do. They guess. All them books they study only tells 'em what things might could be. Just trial and error. And I can guess just as well as they can." His leg never regained feeling, save the aching that went bone deep every time the weather changed, so he dragged it across the house and across the yard and lifted it into bed each night. That's when the bulk of the pecan harvesting fell to his oldest boy, Pecan. His birth name was Thomas, but after the fall, he became Pecan and no one had called him Thomas since.

It was a Stuart pecan tree, the finest, he'd been taught. Straightest, strongest, and meatiest of all the nuts. And it was the crux and core of his family. As far back as Pecan knew, it had always been there in the front yard, planted by nature and not by man. His great-great-grandparents watched it grow from shaggy seedling to bawdy teenager. They knew it would be important one day. His grandparents tended it as it grew from naivety to maturity, and then his parents took over after they died and nurtured it into productivity.

"Just like you, son," Manny had told him. "You're just a scrawny sapling now, but someday you'll be important."

Now, it fell to Pecan to keep the tree healthy, despite its age.

"Pecan trees don't want to die," his father taught him. "Ever seen a pecan stump? Those shoots start reachin' out and beggin' to be a tree again. And if you let 'em alone, they will be. Only a fool would kill a pecan tree. Don't you be that fool, son."

They depended on the pecan tree for extra money during the hard months, but then again, weren't all the months hard? Every fall, Manny would listen out for the unmistakable thud of pecans falling from the trees and hitting the tin roof. He'd head out in the yard to the old barn and grab the wadded-up old bedsheets or tobacco sheets and shake out the dust, then he'd spread them out beneath the foliage for several days to catch the pecans as they fell. Every couple of days the whole family would go out with bags and buckets or whatever container they could find, and on hands and knees they'd brush the curled brown leaves aside to harvest the pecans. Some years were bountiful, some scarce. The Stuart had to take some years to rest, his grandmother told him. Every woman needs a season to rest, she'd say.

Harvesting pecans was time-consuming. Each pecan had to be inspected. A small black speck meant that a worm had already gotten inside the shell and closed the hole back up with his own dung. An open hole meant that the worm had been inside, eaten his fill, and made his way back out again. Either way, holes were bad. Too heavy meant too wet, and too light meant the meat was rotten. The perfect Stuart was caramel in color and bore the strong black stripes of a tiger.

"Look at your skin, baby," his grandmother guided him. "That's the color of the perfect pecan. And don't you ever forget it."

The inferior pecans weren't discarded. They served as coal for fire fodder, or when cracked, they made a good fill for the potholes in the muddy driveway. The worthy Stuarts were taken to the hardware store, weighed, and payment was given accordingly. It wasn't much, but it helped. What helped the most, though, was shelling and selling the pecans themselves. It was painstaking and slow and dirty work, first cracking the armor so as to not damage the nut inside, then cleaning out the creases of narrow innards with the awl. Many weeks were spent sitting on the front porch with a metal tub in their laps shelling, cleaning, and packaging the meat into small burlap sacks for sale. Shelled, whole pecans were worth far more than the unshelled, and Pecan had learned to always stash a few bags in the pantry to save for themselves. It was selfish, really, but his grandmother made the best pecan pie he'd ever wrapped his lips around. Sometimes she would add chocolate shavings to the pie at Thanksgiving.

Toward the end of the season, other pecan tree farmers would pay Pecan a couple of bucks to scale their trees and shake the limbs, trying to capitalize on any nuts still left in the trees. It helped. Anything helped.

Pecan was awake and listened to the December wind blow, and another limb landed on the roof. He pulled the cane-bottomed chair back from the table and walked the few steps to the bedroom to make sure it hadn't woken the children. It was an especially cold night, and they layered all the quilts they owned to stave off the shivering while they slept. Miranda, Pecan's wife, was nestled around their youngest, Mariah. Daniel slept with his grandfather, one stockinged foot peeking out from the quilts. Their faces were burrowed under the blankets, and Pecan was satisfied that they were warm. He left their bedroom door open, stoked the smoldering flame in the fireplace and tossed in some rotten pecans, and walked back to the kitchen.

Christmas was coming, and the children were hoping for a present. He opened the cabinet and counted the sacks of pecans. Four. He could sell three of them, but Miranda would want to keep one for her pies. It wouldn't be much. Maybe enough for one gift for each of them. He'd have to think of something else for his wife and father. He'd check at the hardware store in the morning to see if anyone had any fallen limbs that needed clearing, or if a farmer needed him somewhere to mend a barn or fix any broken machinery. It would help.

He heard the hound dog bark again outside. He'd been barking for a while now, so Pecan lit the lantern on the table and walked to the door to see about the commotion. He braced himself for the cold wind he expected to hit him, but it was still. The sleet and snow mixture fell on the pecan tree and shushed the night like an old school marm. He couldn't see his dog, so he whistled. The tan dog appeared obediently from the dark and trotted up the steps to the porch. Pecan held the door open for him, but the dog wouldn't come in.

"Get in here, ya ole fool. It's cold and wet out there. Why ain't you under the porch? Ain't you got enough sense to get out of the weather?" The dog looked up at him but wouldn't budge. "There's nothin' out there for ya tonight, fella. Come on in." He clicked his tongue like he was nudging a horse. "I ain't gonna stand here with the door open all night, now. Come on!" He raised his voice in authority, but the dog dropped his head and walked slowly back down the steps into the yard. He poised himself in his hunting position and barked again in the same direction. Pecan called again, but this time the dog did not break his stance.

It was unusual for the dog to disobey. Pecan lifted his lantern and squinted in the same direction his dog pointed its nose. He could see nothing through the sleet and darkness, until he caught something through a distant patch of trees. A light? No. Couldn't be. It was probably just a reflection of the lantern on the ice and snow. He listened again but only heard the sound of sleet and the whistle of the faraway train that came through Rennert this time almost every night. The dog barked again, louder now and more frequently, sure of something, but Pecan didn't know what. He left the dog at his watch, closed the door against the cold, and sat down again at the kitchen table.

Pecan looked at the clock that read 1:25 a.m. and reached for his Bible. He heard his grandmother's voice. *If you ever feel uneasy, if you hear the whisper inside of you that tells you something is wrong, pray. And if you don't know what to pray for, read the Word. God will speak to you. All you have to do is pay attention.*

He noticed the caramel color of his arm. *That's the color of the perfect pecan*, he remembered her saying.

Someday you'll be important, his father had said. He turned to the bedroom to see if it was truly his father's voice or a ghost that had somehow slipped past the gate of his rationality.

The dog outside kept barking.

Pecan's fingers moved slowly, partly from the cold and partly from fear of what must be coming. This wasn't the first time he had followed his grandmother's advice. It was really the only time he ever read the Bible, he was ashamed to admit, when he felt uneasy and like something needed to be told. Like when he had been trying to decide whether Miranda was the woman he ought to marry.

He loved her, he knew, but he also knew love meant different things to different people. He had seen it too many times before: One man thought love meant he could go where he wanted to go whenever he wanted to, and when he got home, his wife would still be there waiting for him. Someone else thought love meant that when her husband was away, she could find love in someone else until he got home again. Some thought love was only love as long as she was still pretty or as long as he was still handsome and slim and earning a paycheck. Some thought love was in how many babies could be made, another medal pinned to a father's chest each time his wife went into labor.

And some, the fools, thought love was joy and happiness. But Pecan knew all of these were wrong. Love was undefinable. Love wasn't a list of rules to follow, it was the rule. It was just a misused word spoken by ignorant people who could never understand its purpose or its core. He preferred the word *devotion*. Could he be devoted to Miranda for the rest of his life, and could she be devoted to him? It had to go both ways, he decided. He felt sure he could be devoted to her—it was her eyes, he knew. The deepest pool of dark water with the brightest light he'd ever seen. It was peace in one simple gaze. And her smile and the way she moved her arms when she glided through the house in her bare feet. He could never be with anyone else again, ever. Yes, *devotion* was the word. But could she be devoted to him? Surely there would be times when the paycheck wouldn't come. There would be times when he said the wrong words and made the wrong decisions. There would come a day when he would no longer be able to climb pecan trees and his perfect caramel skin would fade and he would grow old and deformed, and what if one day he could no longer walk? What if he got sick and could never leave his bed again? Would she feed him? Cover him with quilts? Wash his forehead with a cool, clean rag? Or would she leave?

If you don't know what to pray for, read the Word, his grandmother had said. So he'd opened the Bible, let his finger choose the page and line, and read aloud. "For what knowest thou, O wife, whether thou shalt save thy husband? Or how knowest thou, O man, whether thou shalt save thy wife?" He had decided then and there that he and Miranda were meant to save each other. That was the ultimate devotion. So they married.

The dog continued barking, more urgently now, and Pecan heard again the approaching mourn of the train whistle wafting through the night, and so he opened the Bible, randomly landing in Revelation, and read, "And I saw the dead, great and small, standing before the throne, and books were opened. Then another book was opened, which is the book of life. And the dead were judged by what was written in the books, according to what they had done."

The train, he heard his grandmother whisper. *Go to the train.*

* * *

The small fires had dwindled to mere flickers around the site of the derailment, having run out of dry things to burn. The passengers of the southbound train huddled around them, starved for any morsel of heat. They sat on salvaged linens, mattresses, and suitcases, draped in blankets and coats and layers of anything available in the twelve-degree night. It was 1:26 a.m. Soldiers stood around the civilians, their inner codes of honor not allowing them to sit complacently among the pity and fear rising in the others. They checked on the elderly and assisted the crew. They stoked the struggling fires and went back and forth from cars, carrying anything dry to burn.

A man jumped up from the mattress, his eyes wide and his gray hair wet with melted snow. "Why are we out here? Why can't we get back on the train? It's freezing out here." He was angry and scared.

"Sir, it's too dangerous for you all to walk to the train in the dark. It's half a mile up the track. Someone would surely fall and get hurt, and then we'd be in a real mess out here in the middle of nowhere. We'll get you back on the train as soon as the crew figures out the best way."

"What if another train comes?" He half yelled and half whispered. "I think I hear a train!"

A soldier tried to calm him. "Sir, everyone's been evacuated from the train. Everyone is safe. The crew is doing what they can as fast as they can. If another train is coming, I'm sure they've been warned ahead of time. There's a protocol put in place for events such as this. There's nothing to worry about. Now, please, if you'll just sit back down. It shouldn't be too much longer before they load us all into the front cars and we'll be underway and warm and dry again." The old man sat down, shivering and unconvinced.

A dog barked in the distance, and the tracks reverberated the sound of metal clanging and torches hissing and boots crunching over the ice. The crew yelled instructions to each other over the din of machination.

"Never thought this is where I'd be settin' a week before the Lord was born," a man drawled. He rubbed his chin where he could feel his whiskers beginning to grow. "Never thought I'd see a storm like this here one either." He hoped someone would break the silence of the small circle of hunched shoulders and dimly lit faces. He wanted to hear a voice—something human, something warm. He could see his breath when he spoke.

"Where you from?" A woman with a northern accent asked kindly.

"Georgia, ma'am. How' bout you?"

"Concord."

"Not sure exactly where that is," he confessed.

"Massachusetts," she answered.

"Hmm. Can't say as I ever been there."

"Well maybe when we get out of this Godforsaken patch of woods, you can catch a train and come to Massachusetts. It's a lovely place."

"Ma'am, no disrespect, but I'm only plannin' to get on a train one more time in my life, and that's to get me outta here. After that, you won't catch this ole boy on a train, not ever again. I'll flap my arms and try to fly before I set foot onto one of these metal deathtraps again."

"Has anyone seen that pastor that was wearing the Harvard jacket? Where'd he get to?" The passengers looked around at each other and into the firelight bouncing off the tree trunks, searching for him.

"I saw him going back to the train," someone answered. "Said he left something important in there."

The frigid temperatures sucked up the conversation like lungs looking for air in a coffin, and the stranded passengers buried their faces again into their blankets and coats. A soldier stirred the fire, and the icy branches rustled overhead. The angels silently swooped down and took their positions.

Chapter Seven

The angels shot their eyes at God,
"Why does this have to be?"
"Trust Me, darlings, trust Me now,
Your faith belongs in Me."
The titans clashed, the wails arose,
Ears clenched between their hands;
"Fly to them, loves, go to them now,
Their pain propels the Plan."

"Approaching Rennert, North Carolina. Logging 1:29 a.m. Coordinates 34 degrees, 46 minutes 55 seconds north and 79 degrees, 6 minutes 19 seconds west," the conductor reported aloud to the engineer. The locomotive forged northward on the icy rails.

"Copy." The low, steady rumble on the tracks was mesmerizing. Then the engineer spotted something. "Was that a light?" he asked as they charged past in a blur at eighty-five miles per hour. The snow was sporadic now, and the countryside was painted with flecks of white and black. "Did you see that?" the engineer asked.

"Looked like someone waving a light …."

"Is that a train?"

"There's another light …."

"Something's on the track up there. Someone's waving a light …."

"What in the …" The engineer reached for the brake and then saw a mass of metal rise like a leviathan beast before him.

***

Pecan Locklear dragged his fingers beneath the words on the page as he read aloud, "'Behold, He is coming with clouds, and every eye will see Him, even they who pierced Him. And all the tribes of the earth will mourn because of Him. Even so, Amen. I am the alpha and the omega, the beginning and the end,' says the Lord, 'who is and who was and who is to come, the almighty.'"

Pecan leaned back in his chair, full. Those were his favorite verses; his fingers fell on them frequently, and it always filled him with the inimitable power of Christ. He closed his eyes and let the warmth swirl within him, and he put his fears away for a different sleepless night. Not this one. He would worry about war and Christmas presents and money and putting food on the kitchen table another night. But right now, he inexplicably felt God. He glanced at the clock: 1:28 a.m., and he knew he would now be able to sleep. He heard the train whistle growing louder, closer.

The dog was barking louder now, and Pecan thought he would try once more to tempt the dog to come inside before he climbed into bed and used peace for a pillow. He unlatched the door and stepped onto the porch, lantern in hand.

"Come on in, pup," he said. "I told you there ain't nothin' out there. It's just the sleet makin' all that racket." He whistled and patted his leg. The dog did not come. "What's eatin' at you, boy?"

The rumble of the approaching train made its way across the fields to the porch steps and up the clapboards of the house and rattled its windows, as it always did during the winter months. The ground was firm now, sitting stoic in the cold weather, and the vibrations traveled farther and harsher. In the summer, though, the wet dark soil and all the things that were bountiful in it sucked up the rain and the sounds of machines and the worries of men and buried them deep in the earth where they belonged. But right now, it trembled.

The dog suddenly stopped barking, and in that instant, the world burst wide open. Pecan dropped to his knees and covered his ears against the deafening detonation. His eyes were squinted shut, and when he opened them, he saw sparks flying high above the pines, and he heard metal giants clashing and thrashing and saw flames through the faraway branches of the pines. The dog bolted under the porch at the sound of the impact and hid.

"Dear God, what is happening?" Pecan said aloud.

Go to the train, his grandmother's voice reminded him.

Pecan retrieved his lantern where it had fallen on the thin layer of snow and ran inside to wake his father.

"Manny!" he whisper-yelled. "Wake up ... Pops, you awake?" He shook him. "C'mon, I need you to listen to me." His father mumbled and sat up in the bed, confused. "There's been a train wreck. I'm going to see if anyone needs help. I need you to get up and stay put in the kitchen until I get back. Don't wake the kids or Miranda. Do you understand?"

Manny nodded and pulled his limp leg out from beneath the quilt and let it fall to the floor.

"Would you mind heating up some water?"

Manny nodded. "Go," he said. "Carry this quilt."

Pecan grabbed his father's quilt from the rumpled bed and ran from the house. Small, sporadic fires flickered through the trees now, and the shrieks and screams weaved their way toward him through the branches. The dog was at his heels, not knowing why but sensing some importance. Pecan ran, his boots crunching in the frozen soil, and he dreaded with his whole heart what he would soon see. Clearing the last tree line, he stopped running. Stunned, he only heard the sound of his own breathing. It was a dream. It had to be. Oh, God, let this be a dream. He surveyed the heaps of twisted metal and the steam rising up from the carnage. The steel rail ties had been lifted from their berths and were gnarled with the weight of destruction. The smell of diesel suffocated him, and then he heard their screams.

***

The collision was a deafening eruption of metal and iron and bones and blood and flesh and glass and steel and steam and earth and dreams and light and darkness. The first car of the northbound train smashed into the fouled cars of the southbound train at such a high rate of speed that it was lifted up and off the tracks, creating an assembly line of cars caving into each other, one after the other like an accordion. The steel and wooden cars splintered on impact, crushing their passengers and smashing with such force as to create a gouge in the earth the length of two football fields. Devastation and ruin and chaos and cries for mercy from the living and from the nearly dead spread through the night air and clung to it for dear life.

Chapter Eight

On December 16, 1943, the first four cars of the Atlantic Coast
Line locomotive No. 8 collided with the empty derailed cars
of the southbound No. 91 at such a tremendous impact, they
telescoped into the size of just one car. The wreck occurred at
approximately 1:29 a.m. near Raft Creek Swamp in the town
of Rennert, a rural farming community in Robeson County,
North Carolina.

The official cause of the accident was a broken coupling and
brake pipe between the second and third cars of the southbound
train. A broken rail on the track then caused the derailment
of the last three cars, heaving them onto the parallel tracks,
thereby blocking the passage of any northbound train. The
derailment occurred at 12:50 a.m., not allowing enough time to
clear the track before the northbound passenger train arrived
at 1:29 a.m. All attempts to warn the approaching train failed.
The northbound train was traveling at an approximate speed
of eighty-five miles an hour upon impact.

An exact estimate of souls lost is disputed in media
reports but falls between seventy-two and seventy-four
most consistently. The injured falls between 180 and 200.
This may or may not include the suicide of the fireman years
after the wreck.

It is, to date, the worst train wreck in North Carolina
history.

Chapter Nine

The silent countryside then shook,
It trembled with the fear
That earth and fallow field and tree
Would swallow every ear.
But screams and howls, demonic yelps
Resounded through the night;
The agony, the " dear God please,"
Found haven in their flight.

In what felt like slow motion, James Merritt heard metal scraping, bending, crunching, crushing. Then silence. Then the nightmare flashed into reality, and the cataract of terror materialized into screams and moans and shrieks impaling him from every direction. He could see nothing but black—didn't know if his eyes were opened or closed; closed, he hoped. Keep them closed, he told himself. Tight.

He felt his heartbeat in his ears and lifted his hand to his forehead. He followed the wet warmth as it spread across his eyes and along the sharp bridge of his nose and to where it pooled in the pockets of his ears. He tried to lift his head but it wouldn't move. His chest was heavy, and when he tried to shift his shoulders, he could feel the smooth vinyl of a passenger seat pinned across him. It was hard to breathe. He stretched his hand out as far as his fingers could reach and found what he thought might be the cuff of a shirt sleeve. He tugged it, hoping for resistance.

"Hello?" he thought he said. He wasn't certain that he spoke. He could only hear ringing and the sound of a thousand birds in his ears. "Hello? Are you there? Is that you, Edwards?" He pulled at the cuff harder. Nothing.

The screams were louder now. James shook the blood from his ears and strained to distinguish where the screaming came from, but it was coming from every direction.

"Help me!" they screamed. "Someone help! Over here!"

James wanted to help them. He wanted to finally do something right and this time to not run away. He wanted to deserve the medal pinned to his chest. He wanted to do something—anything good— for his father and his mother and for Meredith and his child that maybe didn't even know he existed and for Ben and for Luther and his fallen comrades and for Edwards, the terrible preacher who would not give up on him, and maybe even for himself. Maybe it would change things. Maybe he could be the hero for once and not the villain. Maybe it wasn't too late.

He shimmied his palms into the space between his chest and the vinyl seat across him and gathered all of his hatred and his rage and his love and his fear, and he pushed. The seat shifted and slid slightly to the side. A thousand sharp pins pricked him as he tried to sit up, so he tried to pull his legs out from beneath things that he couldn't see. They wouldn't budge. He reached above his head to get his bearings and felt the jagged edges of metal pointing down at him. He was in a tomb. He felt again for the shirt sleeve and followed it up to the chest and over sharp shards of metal until he found the neck and felt for a pulse. There was none. He felt the person's face but couldn't determine who it was in the dark. He hoped it wasn't Edwards. He needed light, and then he remembered seeing Edwards put his matches in his front shirt pocket, so James felt for it. *Please don't be there*, he thought. *Don't be Edwards.* His fingers were shaking when they hit the small box of matches in the corner of the pocket. "Don't be him," he said aloud.

He pulled the matches out and trembled as he struck the sulfur several times. Finally there was light.

He lifted the flame above his head and saw the nightmare he had warned himself against. This was no longer a train car, but a contorted box of wood and metal. The ceiling was only inches above his head. Nothing was discernible. Beside him was a man's gray hat, a splintered suitcase—and then he saw an arm. He tried to lead the dwindling light to the body, but there was no body. It was a woman's arm, slender and pale with an emerald on her finger. His stomach revolted at the gruesome sight, and he turned his head to vomit. The tips of his fingers burned from the dying match and he quickly turned to identify the corpse beside him. Edwards.

The flame went out, and James didn't want to see any more.

He left his hand on Edwards's chest, still clutching the matches.

"How do you pray, Edwards? You never got around to telling me that. I would pray for you right now, pal, but I don't suppose you need it. I didn't mean what I said about you being a lousy preacher. You're a good preacher. A good man. And I'm glad we met. I'm glad we talked. And I'm sorry that it was you instead of me. It should've been me." The blood on his cheeks was slick and gel-like. "We both know it should've been me. I'm gonna try and remember what you told me. I may not get it right at first, but I'm gonna try, pal.

"In here!" James yelled. He howled and beat his fist on the metal walls, his flesh making no sound and his voice lost in the din of the demonic shrieks and shrills of the other passengers as they were beginning to understand their plight. He felt around for a metal object and found a rod from a seat. He banged the ceiling and the walls and whatever hard thing he could find, terrified that this would become his tomb, terrified that he would never be able to make good on his promise to the preacher.

He was getting cold now, and the caved-in sides of the car were freezing to the touch. He heard nothing but chaos outside: Voices wailed, frantic footsteps crunched in the sleet, mangled passengers moaned and wept.

A man yelled out, begging for someone to shoot him. *Anyone, please shoot me.*

A woman cried for someone to save her unborn baby; her legs were pinned, and she screamed over and over again that she would not lose this child. *I will not lose this baby,* she sobbed. *Not this one too.*

But no one was coming for James. No one answered his calls. No one would be looking for him. *I deserve this,* he thought. *I deserve every moment of this.*

Dizzy, he laid his head down again, knocking the bar against the crumpled metal wall intermittently, just in case. He thought of Michael and Luther on the last night they were alive, and he wished he had fought like Michael. He had never thrown himself in front of a bullet like that for another person. He heard Luther's voice. *Forgiveness, boys, is a beautiful thing.*

Yes, he thought, *for those who can have it.*

He thought of Meredith and how much he wanted the chance to show her that he could be a good man. He could love her now. He couldn't love her then because he hadn't known what it meant, what it felt like, or what it was supposed to feel like. He only knew that if you needed things to fill up the empty spaces within you, there were plenty of things to be found, but eventually they all just create more emptiness. But if love is what you feel when you're sick to your stomach about how you've treated someone, or how you want to do anything within your power to make someone else feel deserving or happy or warm or safe, then maybe he was beginning to understand how to love. When you want to throw yourself in front of a train to kill the shame of all the things you've done, but then you can't do it because you want the chance at love, when even just the chance of it is suddenly enough, then maybe he was getting close. This was his train. This was his sepulcher, and he had to get out.

James closed his eyes and kept his hand on Edwards's chest, patting him. "Should've been me, buddy. Should've been me," he said. His voice was hollow and tinny in the cold air. "You're probably up at the pearly gates by now, huh? Are they really pearly gates? I mean, you wouldn't think God would want to be gaudy. Seems like God would want more of a big wooden barn door. And just on the other side would be those green pastures that some verse says to lie down in. I can't remember the verse. They used to say it a lot in church when I was a kid. Mom would make sure my shoes were shined up and my hair was shined down." He smiled at the memory. "That's when I was a good kid."

The tears rolled from the corner of his eyes and down his temples and into his hair. They were warm, and they felt good. It felt like part of his insides were escaping, coming out to show people all the things that were really going on inside.

"I'm gonna try to pray now, Edwards. I mean, what could it hurt, right? I can't remember the last time I prayed, and if I did, it was only because someone told me to and told me what to say. They weren't my words." He cleared his throat and tried to take a deep breath, then winced at the pain it caused in his ribs.

"So, God, this is James Merritt; it's been a while, if ever, really, and I am a terrible man. I've pretty much done all the things that You told us not to do. You're probably wondering why I'm praying. Why I even dare to speak to You. Well, it's because I just want You to know that I'm sorry, and that I'm going to try to be better. I don't expect You or anyone else to forgive me, even though Edwards here says You'll want to. I don't understand that. I wouldn't be able to forgive me. But I do have a question, or maybe it's a request, although why would You grant me a request? I don't even know what I'm saying. Well, my question is basically about all these other people on this train. Why are they here? They're good people, and there are mothers and fathers and grandparents and people who want to do things with their lives, and there are soldiers who are just trying to get home to see their families after all they've been through in the war. Why are they suffering here? Why can't there be a train full of bad people and a train full of good people, and then You can run my train off a cliff. You can do anything, they say, so why not that? Why cram the good and bad people all together and make everybody suffer all the same, and all their families suffer, when they don't deserve it? I just don't understand the justice of that. So I'm saying that if You need a life … if You have to meet a certain quota tonight, then take me. Amen."

He turned his face to Edwards one last time.

"How'd I do? Geez, I'm even lousier than you are," he patted Edwards's chest again. "Not sure if I'll see you up there or not. I suppose it depends on how gracious He's feeling at the moment. But I did what you said to do. I told Him, so soon I'll either be knocking on the big barn door, or I'll be screaming with my demons for the rest of eternity. Or am I already there?"

Chapter Ten

The angels hurried, flurried 'round,
"Get this one, that one there!
You hold his hand, I'll catch his soul,
He'll go to the land most fair!"
Their wings created such a wind
That parted earth and skies,
So that the dead and dying watched
With unbelieving eyes.

Pecan ran to the first body he saw strewn beside the tracks. It was an old woman.

"Ma'am," he called to her, "are you okay?" He knew it was a stupid question, but it was the only one that would form itself into words.

The old woman's eyes were closed, and her pink cashmere sweater was ripped and matted with blood and mud. She turned her face to him. He knelt over her, not caring that his tears fell on her cheeks.

"Are you okay? Ma'am?"

She opened her eyes slowly. They were gray, and fear flew out of them like a flock of chimney swifts at dusk. She reached for him, and he gave her his hand. She was trembling.

"You've been in a train wreck, ma'am. Do you know where you are?"

She just stared at him.

"You're in Rennert, North Carolina. Can you tell me your name?" he asked.

"Mary Lou," she whispered.

"Well, Mary Lou, looks to me like you're alive, and I think you're gonna make it, okay? You hear me? You're gonna be okay." He tried to lace his words with hope, and he took the quilt draped over his shoulder and wrapped it around her, carefully tucking it beneath her frail frame. "I'm going to get you some help, okay?"

"Wait. Don't leave. What's your name?" she winced with pain.

"Pecan."

"Pecan? That's a funny name," she smiled, her teeth pink with blood. "I like it. Better than Toby."

"Yes, ma'am. Listen, I need you to sit tight while I go get you some help."

"It's okay, Pecan. Go help someone else. If I die, I die. Thy will be done."

"Now don't talk like that, ma'am, you're going to be fine."

"That's not your decision, young man. It's His. I'll be right here; don't have much of a choice anyway. Now you go on and help someone else. Go."

He reluctantly left the old woman and found the next body only a few steps away, a soldier. He looked like he had led and lost a siege on a battlefield, muddy and bloody and eyes wide open and shell-shocked. He was crying silently.

"Sir," Pecan approached him quickly. "Sir, how can I help you? What hurts?" As he said it his eyes dropped to the man's shoulder, and saw he was missing his arm.

The soldier made eye contact with Pecan and held his gaze. He never spoke; he just stared at Pecan until he huffed his last short, staccato breath.

Pecan reached to close the man's eyes for him and left his hand resting there. "Lord, take him," he whispered.

It is surreal to watch a man die, Pecan thought. He never thought of a life as such a tangible thing. *Life*. It had always been just a word. A way to be. We were either alive or we were dead. But to watch this thing that had always just been a word leave its vessel was inexplicable. A dark magic. Like something he was never meant to see. To watch the color drain away from a face so quickly and to watch a spirit lift and flutter and flit from the eyes, leaving only a hollow, vacuous void ... to see the facial muscles relax and the hairline sag in only a quick a moment ... to see the warm, moving miracle of man become a stump in an instant ... to not be able to peer inside a chest to see that a heart has stopped beating or that lungs have stopped breathing, but to know, still, that life had left, was almost too much to grasp. Pecan looked away from the soldier, and he finally understood what his grandmother had tried to teach him about the soul. Just another word, he always thought. *Soul. Life*. He had been so wrong.

***

Mary Lou closed her eyes and thought of Milton. She tried to picture his face looking down on her now, and she strained to hear his voice. "I don't know, Sugar Lump," she answered aloud, shaking her head. The back of her head was wet and cold from the ground, but the quilt kept the rest of her dry from the waning sleet. She couldn't stop shivering, and she could see her white breath in the black air. "That depends on Him. But I wouldn't mind it so much. I sure did want to hold Toby, though. I don't know what to do. Do I stay to hold Toby, or do I go to hold you?" She paused a moment. "Not my decision, Lump, but I do have a preference. Thy will be done. Thy will be done," she repeated over and over again.

***

Men were running now, back and forth among the wreckage and barking orders at each other in panicked voices.

"Who the hell knows we're here," a passenger yelled. "Who knows? We're out in the middle of nowhere!" He threw his head back to the sky and clenched his fists and cried out.

"The ACL's been notified," one crewman injected into the throng of confusion. "Someone in Rocky Mount received our telegram and said he knew some people from these parts, so people are already on the way."

"How soon before they get here? People are dying!"

"Not soon enough," came the dejected answer.

Pecan heard the hoarse pinch of a baby's cry. He followed the sound to a crushed car and dropped to the ground to peer through the broken window. He had forgotten his lantern in his rush to run, and the small fires were not enough to bring light to this darkness. A man ran by with a torch and Pecan yelled to him.

"Sir, your torch! I need your torch! There's a baby in here!"

The man brought the light to Pecan. It was a pine bough with its tip on fire and the sticky sap dripping down the limb.

"Here!" Pecan directed the man to where he found the baby. Pecan was on his stomach, jagged shards of glass slicing into his arms as he stretched through the window to reach the child.

"God, no. No, no, no!" he raged. The child cried again as Pecan pried him out from his mother's mangled, motionless arms.

The man with the torch was speechless, and Pecan had no time for words. He tucked the crying baby under his shirt and coat against his skin to warm it and hurried for home. Miranda would know what to do. He stepped past Mary Lou and he could see that she was still shivering under the quilt, though her face looked calm and resolved.

***

Mary Lou didn't see Pecan rush past with a baby. Her eyes were closed and she was talking to her husband. "I can't move, Lump," Mary Lou said to the sky. "Everything hurts. I just want to sit up. That's all. I just want to sit up and see what happened. Did you see it? You always said I was nosy. Well, you're going to have to tell me all about it. I think it might've been real bad. Can you hear them all crying? I'm going to try not to cry." She closed her eyes and there was a searing heat that flashed across her brain. She tried again to move her arms and legs, but the quilt was too heavy. "They won't stop screaming. I can't hear you, Lump, because they won't stop screaming. Can you hear me? I bet you can. That very nice young man gave me a blanket. That was right sweet of him. I can't remember his name, though. He told me, but it wasn't Toby. I was just trying to go to see our Toby. I just want to squeeze his little fat rolls. That's all I wanted. But here I am. Thy will be done," she whispered again. "I understand. Yes, I understand." She closed her eyes and the corners of her mouth curved up, then she pursed her lips together, raised her chin, and kissed the air three times.

* * *

Pecan burst through the door and found his father sitting at the kitchen table.

"Where's the water? We need a rag with warm water!" His father had not yet seen the child under Pecan's dirt- and blood-smeared coat but answered his son's hysteria by obeying. He dragged himself to the sink to get the washrag and dipped it in the pot of water on the stove.

Pecan had taken off his jacket and spread it out on the table like a blanket. He undressed the child—a boy—and checked that the rag wasn't too hot and began wiping the baby clean of the smeared blood, and as he did this, the baby quieted.

Miranda appeared in the doorway. A chill ran through her even though her nightgown was long and flannel. "I thought I heard a baby," she said, walking over to them.

"You did," Pecan answered. "It's awful, Miranda, just awful …."

"What's awful? Whose child is this? What's happened to him?"

"The train crashed … I heard the most God-awful explosion …" He was breaking now. His voice quivered as he tried to explain, and he put his fist to his nose to stifle the sobs.

Miranda saw the gashes on her husband's arms and went for another rag.

"There are bodies everywhere and people missing arms and legs, and it looks like a bomb went off and people were thrown everywhere!" He was sobbing.

Miranda held his arms down, smoothed his hair from his forehead with the rag, and made him sit in a chair to calm down. "Manny, make him some coffee." She took the wet rag and blotted the wounds on his arms. "Where is his mother?"

"Dead."

"Father?"

"I don't know. I don't know where anyone is. I just heard a baby screaming and I found him and I saw his dead mother and I didn't know what to do. It was freezing out there and he was cold and scared and it was dark and I couldn't see anything but that his mother was dead. There was only half of her." Pecan took the rag from Miranda and held it against his wild eyes. He closed them in an attempt to unsee the carnage he had just witnessed.

His father brought him a cup of coffee and laid his hand on his back to calm him.

"The tracks are twisted up like a bag of pretzels, and people were screaming and begging for help. I saw an old woman who was still alive and all I could do was put a quilt around her. I don't even know if she's still alive or not." His hand trembled as he brought the coffee to his mouth, and some of it sloshed onto the table.

"A soldier took his last breath right in front of me," he continued, "and what was I supposed to do? Then I heard the baby and I knew we had to get the baby warm. I didn't know what else to do. I just took the baby and started running." His head was in his hands now and his voice broke with the telling.

"Pecan, you got to settle down. You did the right thing, hear? You saved this baby," she said as she gently touched the child's cheek. "He's safe now. He's safe and warm. Now settle down. Let me take a better look at him." Her fingers investigated every inch of him. "It's amazing. None of this blood is his own. I don't see any injuries on the little guy, not a mark, not a cut. Mama did her job. She protected him. She saved his life." She picked up the baby and cradled him against her chest and turned back to her husband. "Now, settle yourself. Take a deep breath. It's going to be okay."

"Proud of you, boy," Manny said.

Pecan tried to sip his coffee and collect himself. He watched his wife comfort the baby, and it comforted him too. She swayed the infant back and forth in a mesmerizing dance, humming a tune to soothe him. She walked to the window and saw the fires through the trees. The dog lay on the porch now, his brown eyes watching and reflecting the lights.

"What'd the train hit?" Manny asked.

"I don't know. Could've been a bomb. Could've been a car. Another train? I don't know. It was just a mangled mess of metal. I couldn't see." He went to the sink to wash his hands and face and forearms.

"I gotta go back. There are so many more people. I need more quilts. Jackets. Sheets. Anything."

"I can help," Manny answered.

"Don't wake the kids," he told Miranda. "I don't want them to see this. Pops, you don't need to be out there in this weather either. You'll catch the croup out there." Pecan gathered quilts from the other bed while Miranda poured the rest of the hot coffee in a large can.

"Well I'm going anyway," Manny insisted. "It's my leg that's broke, son, not my humanity."

***

The rescue men with the acetylene torches knelt by one of the crushed train cars and commenced to carve through the mangled frame.

"There's no way anyone in this car survived," they said to each other. Their hearts were heavy, and they shook their heads and commenced to recovering dead bodies and the parts of them.

"Wait, be quiet for a second," one of the men said. "Listen."

The torches stopped and they flipped their shields up to expose their ears. The sounds of vehicles and yelling and hissing and sobbing gushed at them, and they wanted to put their shields back down and drown it all out again.

"No, wait. I hear something!"

Faintly, a knock came from inside of the car. They listened again to be sure of what they heard, and another knock, weak and puny, escaped from inside.

"Someone's alive!" a couple of men shouted out and ran to retrieve the doctors while the men with the torches bent to their task with urgency.

Inside the car, James heard their voices. They were close now, and he could hear the high-pitched sound of steel and fire colliding, and he could feel the heat. He tried to open his eyes; flashes of sparks and a fine line of red were just beyond his reach. *Someone's alive*, he heard them say. But was he? The iron bar fell from his hand and landed with a thud beside him. Was he? He felt hot inside, like those torches were cutting though his flesh and bone, and he couldn't keep his eyes open anymore. He tried to picture his parents, and he saw his mother's face smiling at him while she combed his hair. He saw his father standing behind her, stern and proud, and he saw his bedroom. The carpet was clean and vacuumed, and his navy blue-and-red plaid comforter had been neatly made and tucked around his small bed. He tried to see Meredith, but he couldn't make out her face. He imagined that he smelled chamomile and wondered if his child was a boy or a girl. He only hoped it wasn't like him. He wanted to go back and do it all over again. To fix things. To say he was sorry and that he was a fool and that he would make it up to all of them. He wanted to try. *Hell no, not try. Do. There will be no more trying, just doing.* He knew now, he thought, what it took to be a man. It takes caring for someone else more than you care about yourself. That's all. Simple as that. That's how he could finally be a man.

He could hear the metal tearing and heard the men yelling frantically, "Here! In here!" Gloved hands peeled the sides of the train back, and faces appeared in the hole. A flashlight beamed in his face, and he realized his eyes must have been open because he squinted at the light.

"Pull the seat off! Get it off of him! There's a man alive in here!"

James winced as the rescuers dragged the debris across his broken body and began to pull him out of the wreckage.

Chapter Eleven

And from the fires scattered there,
Satan then arose.
He breathed a breath of grief and death
And reveled in their woes.
The wails and moans and ghastly tones
Were music to his ears.
He laughed and danced and licked his lips,
"My sinners, I am here."

Time was as frozen as the ice that wrapped itself around the buckled steel rails. The fireman on locomotive No. 91 sat in the middle of the steaming rubble, sobbing. Through blurry, bloodshot eyes, he surveyed the littered bodies, the twisted rails, the splintered tombs sprawled across the wet, frozen ground. The only source of light was the glinting of the small fires that hopped and jabbed and stabbed across the scene of devastation.

If only he had not slipped, he thought. If only he had not slipped and broken the fuse on the tracks, none of this would have happened. None of these people would be dead. *I did this.*

The engineer saw him and knelt down beside him.

"Come on, buddy, let's get you dry. Let's get you over here by the fire." He put his hand under the fireman's elbow to help him up.

The fireman, like a madman trapped in a mental cage soldered shut by his own guilt, jerked his arm away and turned savagely to the engineer. "I can't."

"You can't blame yourself for this, Jake. This wasn't your fault."

"How can you say that?" The spit flew from his mouth as he yelled. "How can you dare say that? I did this! I fell! That was me!" He pounded his own chest. "I slipped and fell and didn't do my job! That was my job! Not yours, not anybody else's, mine! And I broke it. I slipped. I couldn't light it. It is my fault. It's all my fault." He dropped his head and his shoulders shook with the sobbing. "I can't live with this. I can't. I won't be able to live with this."

The engineer waved another crewman over to help him, and they dragged the fireman toward the nearest fire. "He's in shock. We need to get him warm."

"No," the fireman protested. He reached up to tear their hands off his coat. "Leave me here. Leave me!"

The engineer would try a sterner approach. "Listen here. I don't have time to babysit a grown man. Now sit by this fire and warm up so you can help me with the survivors. Stop blaming yourself and do something. You couldn't help the ice and you couldn't help slipping. Just like none of us could help the brakes freezing up or the coupling breaking or the rail breaking or the fuse breaking. It broke on all of us. All of us. Now sit here for a minute and get it together. We still have work to do. I telegraphed the ACL in Rocky Mount. They're sending help now. The operator knows exactly where we are—grew up around here or something like that. They'll be here any minute. Now come on, we've got to get these people near the fires or they'll freeze to death, those that aren't dead already."

***

The Robeson County coroner was sleeping when he heard the telephone ring in the middle of the night. He slipped his robe over his pajamas and hurried to the kitchen, fumbling the earpiece as he lifted it from the wall.

"Hello?" It wasn't the first time he'd received a desperate call in the middle of the night. It was all a part of the job description. He listened to a man's voice on the other end of the line. "Jesus. Raft Creek Swamp. Yes. I'll be there as fast as I can." He hung up the phone and immediately called his son.

"William, come pick me up right now. There's been a train wreck in Rennert. Bring the ambulance from the funeral home." He hung up quickly to avoid any questions that might delay his son's departure, then made several other calls to those who could help, including some local veterinarians.

The exact locale was difficult to find. The railroad tracks were well off the main road, and the pelting rain and sleet made visibility and navigating the ambulance difficult. Finally seeing the fires, the men directed the ambulance in that direction. Its tires splashed through the partially frozen puddles and found the grooves of a farm road that ran parallel to the tracks. It looked like Armageddon. The train cars were strewn like branches after a storm, some on their sides, and three of them telescoped into one. Bodies were everywhere. Some people were dragging themselves slowly out of the mud, and many people were not moving at all. Scattered luggage littered the scene, and scraps of garments hung in the nearby trees.

The coroner jumped out of the car and ran to the first injured people he saw, waving his son to drive closer to help load them.

"We can only fit three!" William yelled to his father.

There were too many people. He didn't know who to help first. The maimed and injured were overwhelming, their cries for help rushing at them like the pricking of icy wind. Debris was scattered as far as the light would allow them to see, and it was difficult to walk among it all.

"Ma'am!" he ran to a woman who was trying to stand. "Come with me. Let's get you to a hospital." Her face and hair were matted in blood, and her eyes were swollen shut. Dazed and silent, she grabbed his extended hand and was led to the ambulance.

"Dad, help me here!" William was trying to lift a man who was screaming in pain, his leg broken and bent backward. They worked frantically, grabbing splintered wooden fragments to use as makeshift splints, their fingers quickly numbing in the cold. With the third injured passenger loaded, William shut the ambulance door and ran back to the driver's seat.

"One more!" William waved an injured soldier to him. "I can fit one more!" He grabbed a soldier who was limping toward him and helped him into the car.

"Taking them to Baker!" William yelled and sped away. Other survivors had seen the lights on the ambulance, and those who could walk were coming toward them and yelling for help as he pulled away.

"More help is coming," the coroner tried to reassure them. "They're coming. They'll be here any minute, folks."

* * *

Pecan and Manny Locklear hurried back to the scene, toting all the blankets they owned and two large cans of coffee that burned Pecan's hands as it sloshed. Manny dragged his leg behind him, his boot leaving a shallow trench in the sodden fields.

At the crash site, Manny stopped and stood frozen, his mouth open and his eyes full. They helped to drag a few passengers closer to the bonfires for warmth, while the train's crewmen and those servicemen not mortally wounded grabbed mattresses from the Pullman sleepers and sheets and clothing from busted luggage and anything else that would provide tourniquets, comfort, or warmth.

Pecan bent down over a soldier whose neck had been slashed and was bleeding heavily. He grabbed a garment from the mud and ripped it to make a bandage and tied it around the soldier's neck to stifle the bleeding.

"You're gonna be okay, soldier. Hear me? You're gonna be okay. We got the bleeding stopped now." Pecan tucked a quilt around him. "Can you tell me your name, sir?"

The soldier could not turn his head, so he moved his eyes instead to Pecan's face.

"Corporal Harold Hendrix."

"Good, Corporal. You're going to be just fine. Hang in there. I just saw an ambulance leaving. More are on the way."

"What hit us? A bomb?"

"No, sir. Not a bomb. You hit another train."

"Casualties?"

Pecan hesitated. "Many," he answered truthfully.

"I have daughters," he whispered. "I can't leave them."

"Then don't. You're gonna be home real soon."

The corporal moved his eyes away and tried to look in the opposite direction. "Where's Mary Lou?"

"I'm sorry, I don't know Mary Lou."

"She was sitting with me on the train. Short, little old lady, gray eyes, sassy."

Pecan remembered the woman with the gray eyes. "I saw her earlier. She was alive."

Corporal Hendrix smiled. "Good for her. She hates the name Toby and the color purple." He grunted with the effort of a chuckle. "Said it was the saddest color on the planet." He coughed, and blood seeped from the corners of his mouth. He looked again at Pecan. "I won't see my girls again, will I? Tell me the truth. I can take it."

"You'll see your girls again," he answered the dying man. "But it won't be today, and maybe not tomorrow. But you'll see them again, all right. Of that, sir, I am certain. Tell me this, Corporal," Pecan tried to keep him there with him. "Who is winning the war?" There was no answer, and Pecan tried again. "I said, who is winning the war, Corporal?" He tried using a military voice.

The corporal turned to him and tried to smile. "We are. We're winning the war." The corporal smiled again, and Pecan watched the life leave the man's eyes and the smile wane from his bloody lips. Then he brought his hand up to his brow and saluted the soldier.

***

Others from nearby towns soon arrived at the gruesome scene, among them Dr. C.T. Jackson and his young son, Charlie. Dr. Richard

MacDonald brought his nurse, Sadie Currie, to assist him. With black leather bags in hand, the doctors went first to those still trapped inside the mangled train cars, those whose animal screams could form no words and arced up high above the other voices pleading for help.

"Ma'am!" Dr. Jackson was on his knees, reaching through a hole in the car where he saw a woman's hand flailing. He grabbed her hand to steady her, and she desperately clawed to hold on to him. He yelled for Charlie to pass him the syringe of morphine. He tried to hold her arm down and find the most accessible vein, but she could not still herself.

"Ma'am, please try to be still. We're trying to help you. I need to give you some morphine to help your pain. You need to be still." She could not understand him or maybe could not hear him over the chaos, and then he saw that her legs had been crushed. "Another syringe!" he yelled to Charles.

He thumped the liquid in the syringe to prepare another shot. The morphine was freezing in the twelve-degree temperature.

"Charlie! We've got to heat these syringes up! Lift the hood on the car and set them near the motor until they thaw. Bring them back as soon as they're liquid again! Hurry!" Charlie grabbed a handful of pre-loaded syringes and a bottle of morphine and did as his father instructed.

Dr. Jackson moved from man to man, woman to woman, dead to dying, doing whatever it was he could do.

"Doctor!" a woman yelled. "Doctor, here! I'm over here! Please, doctor," her voice fell to defeat. Dr. MacDonald heard her.

"I'm here, ma'am. I'm here." He grabbed her wrist and turned it to take her pulse. Her heart was racing and he had to settle her down.

"Take my baby," she whispered. Her voice was hoarse from shouting. "Please, I'm eight months pregnant. Take it now. Cut me open and save my baby."

The doctor saw that she was pinned beneath splintered boards, only her torso and head exposed. She put his hand on her belly. "Please," she begged. "Save my baby. This, this is my husband," and she placed her hand on a man's face that was still and gray beside her. "It's all I have left of him."

Dr. MacDonald shook the horror and empathy from his heart and braced himself with trained rationality.

"Ma'am, I cannot do that. Your baby is in the safest place he can be in right now." He tried to sound sure and stopped the trembling in his voice. "If I take him now, he may die of exposure before we could get him to a hospital. If anything goes wrong, we can't help him out here. But you are alive. Your blood is pumping and you are keeping him warm. You can save your baby far better than I can. Now stay with me. We're going to get you free very soon. The men are here with the acetylene torches, and they're going to get you out. Can you hold on for me? For your baby?" He held her hand and squeezed it.

"Yes, doctor. I can. I will," and she settled her head back down, tightened her jaw, and set her resolve to survive.

"Sadie," the doctor called his nurse. She was busy wrapping a man's head in gauze. "We need another blanket here. This woman's pregnant."

"Doc, we don't have any more blankets."

"Try the trunk of my car. There may be something in there. Grab anything you see."

Sadie secured the man's gauze by tucking it into itself. "You're going to be fine, honey," she said to the man. "I hear the ambulance coming, and I'll be right back to help you, okay?"

She ran to retrieve whatever she could find from the doctor's car. A man in a makeshift stretcher of knotted sheets was carried past her, and she had to step over several bodies that had clawed their way out of the wreckage and lay gasping in the mud. Hands reached up for her ankles as she passed. She turned the key in the trunk and found a black wool coat, an umbrella, and a small box of cola bottles. She grabbed the coat and the sodas and noticed a Graham's department store gift box. She opened it and unfolded the tissue paper inside. It was a brand-new woman's long box coat, bright fuchsia. A Christmas present for the doctor's wife, Sadie assumed. She grabbed the black and pink coats, draped them over her arms, and turned to rush back to the doctor. Dodging a jagged piece of metal on the ground, she turned too quickly and slipped on the ice. The bottles crashed as she fell, and the coats buffered her fall. Writhing, she grabbed her ankle and saw the bone protruding from the side. It was broken.

"No," she shouted, furious at herself. She caught her breath and steeled herself against the sharp pain radiating through her ankle and foot and up to her knee. She pulled herself to standing, gathered up the coats, and limped gingerly to the doctor. He was with the pregnant woman. The doctor grabbed the black coat and Sadie jerked it back.

"No," she said. "She gets this one," and she held up the fuchsia coat. He looked at her incredulously.

"But that was for my wi—"

"I know," she interrupted. "But this woman needs it more." She kneeled and bent over the woman. "Look at this coat," she said, draping the coat over the mother's stomach and shoulders. "Isn't it beautiful? And you're beautiful, and that baby of yours will be beautiful too." The woman smiled and nodded.

Sadie winced in pain and grabbed her ankle.

"What happened?" the doctor asked.

"Slipped. It's broken."

"Then you need to get to the hospital," he urged. "You can't work out here with a broken ankle."

"I can work out here with a broken ankle better than I can work sittin' in a hospital. I'll tend to it when I can, but right now these people need more help than I do. Besides, this cold will keep the swelling down."

"Sadie, you can't …"

"Doc, you couldn't drag me out of here if you tied me to a mule."

Dr. MacDonald had learned long ago that when Sadie made up her mind about something, that was that.

"Let's at least get it splinted then," he acquiesced.

Acetylene torches brightened the night, and the sounds of them slicing through metal muffled the moans of the living and the dying. The sparks splashed up like cascades against boulders, and the men behind goggles and gloves called out when they had cut an opening big enough to bend back metal and pull out a victim.

Headlights bounced on the bumpy road as ambulances and hearses serving as ambulances made their rounds carrying as many injured as possible to different locations. The first to surpass capacity was Baker Sanatorium in Lumberton. Doctors worked through the night, the hallways stacked and mobbed with those needing urgent medical care. The staff was only half capacity since several local doctors were sent to the war front, and some train victims bled to death in the hallways waiting for help. Worse, there was no penicillin available—it, too, had been shipped out to the front lines. The sanatorium had only sulfa to treat the grisly open wounds.

Funeral homes in the surrounding towns were soon transformed into makeshift medical facilities. Red Springs Funeral Home was closest to the accident, and both the living and the dead were sent there to await their fates. The dead were kept there until they could be identified, if they could be identified. Many victims were decapitated when the train cars telescoped. Nurses kept logs of any identifiable characteristics: types and sizes of shoes, colors and kinds of clothing, rings and jewelry and watches, birthmarks and scars and the occasional tattoo.

By now the locals had heard of the atrocities, and as all small towns do, they came together at the allegiance of their blood and their land and their morals and their upbringing, and they opened their homes to those who had none there. It would take days or weeks or months for most of the travelers to be well enough to make their way back to their own hometowns.

***

Dr. Jackson brought a soldier into his own home. The man's wool Pullman blanket was wet and dripping over his shoulders as the doctor sat him down at the kitchen table before he returned to the accident again. Mrs. Jackson poured him some coffee and gave him a dry blanket.

"What's your name, son?" Mrs. Jackson asked.

"Thomas. Thomas Valenti. From upstate."

"Are you hungry?"

"No, thank you. Can't eat right now." He stared blankly at his cup of coffee.

Mrs. Jackson spooned the sugar in his cup for him, seeing that his hands trembled in his lap, and stirred.

"We need to try to warm you up, honey. Can you try to drink this?" She inched the cup closer to him. He didn't answer.

"Charlie," she called to her son. "I want you to go on up and wash your face and get on some dry clothes, okay?"

"Yes, ma'am," he obeyed.

"Charlie? Come here." She studied his face and cupped his chin to get a better look at him. "Are you okay?"

Charlie hesitated. "Yes, ma'am. I'm okay," he lied.

But the truth was that he didn't want to be back at home in his warm pajamas drinking warm milk. He wanted to go back to the accident with his father. It was the worst, most gruesome thing that he had ever seen in his twelve years of life, but it was the most important thing too. He didn't know there could ever be suffering like this in his own backyard and from people all over the place and from towns he had never heard of. Strangers had to depend on each other all of a sudden, like the one in his house now.

Charlie didn't know that sometimes brave soldiers got scared and needed help, too, and that he could be the one to help them. He didn't know that someone could lose a leg or an arm or a foot or a hand and still be alive, or even still want to be alive, all because they didn't want to die. That happened, didn't it? Isn't that what he saw? Didn't he see the woman without a leg saying she had to get home to her children? Didn't he see that man missing an arm wrapping a sheet around himself to try to stop the bleeding so he could find his wife in the wreckage?

But not everyone felt that way.

Some people, he recalled, were begging to die. He had heard the yelling from inside the train—*Shoot me*! They were pleading with the doctors or the soldiers to shoot them right there on the spot, just like his uncle had to shoot a lame heifer once in the pasture. Some people didn't want to try; they just wanted to be left alone to die.

Maybe they don't have anyone to go home to like I do, Charlie thought. But he didn't want to be at home in a warm bed looking out of his window with frost gathered in the corners of the panes and a mug of hot chocolate on his bedside table. He wanted to be on the other side, in the cold, wet mud helping these people. He would be like his father someday, he promised himself. He would be a doctor someday and help people.

His mother kissed the top of his head and brushed the bangs back from his forehead.

"I'll make you a sandwich if you're hungry when you're done washing up."

"I want to go back and help Dad," he said.

"Oh no, honey. You can't go back out there. It's too awful."

"I know it's awful; that's why he needs my help. I can help him."

She cupped her hands on his cheeks and drew him closer to her face. "Charlie, there are some things that children shouldn't see. Your father didn't want you to see any more of that carnage. He wanted you to be home and safe. If you want to help your father, put his mind at ease by letting him know that his best boy is safe and sound and far away from that train."

"Yes, ma'am," he dropped his head and went to his room without a sandwich or hot chocolate.

***

Mrs. Jackson went back to the table and sat with the soldier in silence. Finally, Thomas took a sip of coffee and spoke.

"It was like the war out there. I thought I was done with the war for a little while." He held his coffee cup with both hands and shivered. "It was like we were hit by a bomb. One minute I'm dozing off, dreaming about fishing for tog at the jetty down from my house, and then boom! Lightning flashed and I'm being thrown through the air and I land outside on the ground. Everything's black and I can't see anything. And I can't find Joe. We grew up together, got drafted together, then we fought together in Italy, got Mussolini kicked out—

we did that together too. We were finally headed home to kiss our wives and hold our babies and get some rest."

"You can still go home, Thomas," Mrs. Jackson said gently.

He looked at her with wet brown eyes. "Yeah, I can. But Joe can't. I couldn't find him."

"I'm sorry, honey. Maybe he made it to a hospital, and that's why you couldn't find him."

"Yeah, maybe," he answered and tightened the blanket around his shoulders.

Chapter Twelve

The devil picked and plucked his souls,
Then said, "But I want more."
He plundered through the embers' ash
In search of those faith-poor.
"You cannot have them yet, you cur,
They're standing at the gate.
They'll face almighty God and kneel,
And then they'll learn their fate."

First light came grim and gray. The winter sky hung low and somber, hovering above the charred train wreckage that lay paralyzed, twisted, and silent. Weak plumes from the smoldering embers rose up half-heartedly from their pyres in a hopeless and obedient prayer, and the ground was grimy with trampled mud and soiled snow. Suitcases, most of them busted open, were being gathered by men in uniforms. Women's blouses and dresses and men's half-folded uniforms and partially shined shoes were put back into the suitcases nearest to them. Christmas presents littered the scene—dolls, toy soldiers with tanks and jeeps, train sets. Festive wrapping paper and ribbons were strewn, soggy and torn, their destinations sad and final.

A wedding dress, light and fresh against the dismal ground, was draped over a twisted steel tie, yards away from its matching veil. Captain Christopher Vaillant knelt over the dress and rubbed the fabric between his fingers. "Ellie," he whispered her name. Fear welled up in his chest.

It was only hours earlier that he had been resting in his bunk at Fort Moultrie, thinking of his bride and their abbreviated honeymoon. She would be a good wife, he had decided. He felt sure that she was pregnant, but he wouldn't know for certain until he returned home. If she wasn't, then she would be by the time he left again. He'd make sure of that. It would be a boy, and he'd be named Christopher William Vaillant Jr. She was a young wife, yes, but being a mother has a way of settling any woman down, and he believed Ellie could use a little settling down. He would train her to be the best of wives. He had made a good choice, he congratulated himself.

He had readjusted his pillow and reviewed the details of his orders and the embarkation that would greet him in just a few hours. He would be ferried to Fort Sumter and board a cruiser for France. He hoped that his men were ready and, most of all, that they were competent. He didn't want to be responsible for babysitting a bunch of greenhorns who'd never left base and trembled when they aimed their rifles. Those were the kind that had nightmares at night and sniveled for their mothers during the day.

His duffel bag was packed, zipped, and poised for departure at the foot of his steel-framed bed when he and the other soldiers were abruptly awakened by the squalling of air horns. They scrambled into their boots and fatigues in less than a minute and stood at attention. Others rushed to their posts and awaited further orders. Spotlight beams scanned past the marsh and across the harbor in search of possible U-boats.

Captain Vaillant reported to Hazardous Energy Control Program. "What's going on?" he demanded.

"Telegram received, sir, stating the wreck of two Atlantic Coast Line locomotives near Fort Bragg. Possible bomb. Possible German interference. All East Coast bases on high alert." Vaillant snatched the flimsy paper and read it for himself.

"Which trains?"

"ACL Number Ninety-one and ACL Number Eight, Tamiami Champion; southbound and northbound collision. What shall I reply, sir?"

But Vaillant was already gone. He was frantically rapping on the glass window of his commander's office.

"My wife is on that train!" he yelled through the glass. He slammed the telegram paper onto the window. "I need immediate transportation to the site. Now!" He would not be denied.

The commander picked up the telephone and spoke a few words, then whipped his finger and pointed the captain away. He stuck his head out of the door as Vaillant rushed away down the hall and called to him, "You have until zero hundred hours, Captain. That's all I can do. The war won't wait. Sir, I hope she's okay." But the telegram pronounced many dead and wounded.

Men in stark military uniforms and black boots infiltrated the site, helping to remove the last of their dead kinsmen and absorbing and documenting the scope of the tragedy. They had come at dawn, armed with the shields of their trained stoicism and solemnity, and as soon as their eyes fell on their fallen, their mission became personal. Dispatched from Fort Bragg in Fayetteville, the army came with truckloads of blankets and food and supplies to help relieve the local housewives and citizens and businesses who had selflessly opened their doors and their homes and their pantries during the night. They sent fresh supplies to the local hospitals and funeral homes that had depleted their shelves in the efforts to help the victims of the Tamiami Champion tragedy.

By dawn, photographers and journalists had heard the news too. They located the rural wreckage site and began to swarm, cameras clicking and pens jotting the gory details of the gruesomeness. Mangled tracks. Smoldering fires. Scars of acetylene torches cut through smashed rail cars. Blood-soaked snow. Telescoped. So many dead. Decapitations. Severed limbs. Children's toys. Christmas gifts. Bridal gown. Soldiers going home for Christmas. Families torn apart.

The Fort Bragg soldiers would have none of it, though. Cameras were immediately confiscated, and the rolls of film were ripped out on the spot. The site was soon blocked off from any media or civilian spectators until the investigation could be completed. For safety reasons, they said. To prevent wartime propaganda, they explained.

Captain Vaillant heard the clicking of a camera behind him as he knelt over his wife's wedding dress.

"What are you doing?" he confronted the photographer.

"*Fayetteville News and Observer*, sir."

"I don't care if you're from the White House. Surrender your camera." He stepped toward the photographer and held out his palm.

"I'm done. Just needed one shot for the front page," he stammered and started to back away.

Vaillant struck like a viper. He grabbed the man by the front of his shirt and took the camera. He shoved the timid journalist into the mud and ice and snatched the film from the camera, throwing it into a heap of burning cinders. Then he hurled the camera as far as he could into the pine trees, glaring at the photographer.

"We said no pictures. You see this?" He bent down and picked up the dress from the snow. "See this? This is my wife's!" He shook the dress at the man. "This is my wife's! And you come out here with your little camera to get a shot of this for your slimy paper? I don't even know if she's alive! And you want a picture? Get the hell out of here!" he roared, and fury flew from his mouth.

The photographer fled for the trees, and the captain fell on his knees in front of the veil. He scooped it with his hands and brought it to his face, trying to catch the scent of Ellie's perfume. He only smelled fumes. A partially burned Bible and a charred tin box were beneath the veil, and Christopher wiped the mud to reveal the gold letters on the bottom: Harvard Divinity.

He scanned the ground nearby, hoping to identify any of her other belongings. He found her purse half opened in the mud several feet away, and when he pulled out her identification and read her name, a pang caught him in the chest. Ellie. His bride. His wife. Did she survive?

He pulled out her lipstick and opened the cap, thinking of the color on her lips just two nights ago. There was her handkerchief, a compact with powder, a mirror, and a single key—the key to their new home. She may never open that door.

He felt in the side pocket and pulled out a ring. It was Ellie's wedding band. He fingered it and slipped it onto his pinkie. "Why would she have taken this off?" he asked himself aloud. "This should have been on her finger. She wouldn't have taken this off."

He dug into the side pockets and the bottom corners of the purse and found only a few coins. "Where is the money I left her?" he asked aloud. He looked around to see if it was nearby in the trampled earth. He gathered her dress and veil and purse and marched to the military jeep. Private Daniels was waiting at the wheel.

"Private, we need a list of all the local hospitals that the survivors were taken to. I think my wife may be alive. I think she's still alive." He looked down again at his wedding band and then hers. But elation and relief weren't what he was feeling. It was confusion. And maybe anger.

* * *

Holding the tiny slip of paper up against the last smudge of daylight, Ellie compared the address written to the number on the door of the big blue house: 208. She double-checked the street: Ranier. This was the place, but she was nervous. It was getting dark quickly, and she had nowhere else to go. She had never done anything like this before. She checked the address again and looked back at the house. It was beautiful. It was two stories, painted blue as a summer sky; windows with distorted wavy glass stretched across the front. A Christmas wreath with blue ribbon and red berries hung centered on the door.

Framed by white shutters, a curtain moved to the side, and the front porch light snapped on. The door soon opened. A tall African American woman stepped out from behind the screen door with her hands on her hips and a kitchen rag thrown over her shoulder.

"Can I help you, miss?" she asked, annoyed.

"Um. Well, yes. I was wondering if this was the McKeller House? I was told there may be a room available to rent here?"

"This is the McKeller House," the woman answered. "But this ain't no nursery, child, and I ain't no nanny."

Nervous, Ellie studied the paper more closely. *McKeller House. Room to let. 208 Ranier Street. Women only. Apply in person.*

"Yes, ma'am. I'm not looking for a nursery. I'm actually eighteen years old, and I don't have any children."

The woman looked at her sideways. "Not no way on God's green earth that you're eighteen. Get your scrawny tail up here and let me look at you in the light."

Ellie obeyed and climbed the steps cautiously.

"Well hurry it up, would ya? I got things to do and it's cold out here. And I already told you, babysittn' ain't on my to-do list. Sit right there," she pointed to a freshly painted white rocking chair. "I'll be right back."

Ellie hoped the curt woman had gone to get the homeowner, someone friendlier maybe. Did she really look that young, she wondered? She was a married woman now, after all. Well, not truly. Not anymore. She still wasn't sure if she had made the right decision by stepping off that train, but it most definitely wasn't the wrong one. This felt good. Being able to speak for herself without her parents or her sister or Christopher hovering over her and interrupting her was invigorating. She could feel her confidence growing.

The African American woman bumped open the screen door with her hip and carried a tray out to sit on the table.

"Here. Have some coffee, little girl." She poured it into a mug and handed it to Ellie. "You are allowed to have coffee, aren't you?"

"Thank you, yes. I told you, I'm eighteen."

"Right. Do you wanna share your name with me?" She leaned back in the other rocker and stared at Ellie, her eyebrows crumpled inquisitively.

"Eleanor McCollum Vai—Eleanor McCollum." Ellie realized too late that she should have used a pseudonym. Frustrated, she averted her eyes to the front door.

"Oh I'm not inviting you inside. I don't care how cold it is. You see, if I invite you inside, you might assume that you're welcome here. And I don't know if I want you to be welcome or not. So we're just gonna sit here on this porch until we get this thing figured out, understand?"

Ellie sipped her coffee and didn't dare suggest that she'd like another cube of sugar. She noticed the woman's straight white teeth and smooth skin stretched over regal cheekbones. She held her head with an elegance that Ellie recalled from her mother's society parties in Charleston. She was quite lovely. "I understand," she answered. "Is the homeowner here by chance?"

The woman flashed a curt smile. "Speaking."

"I'm sorry," Ellie stuttered. "I didn't realize …."

"I know you didn't realize. You're too busy thinking what's an African American woman doin' owning an establishment like this one, right? Well, I'm gonna tell you. I am Miss Betty Bethea, I am twenty-nine years young, and I am indeed runnin' my own business. I have spent every day of my life working these hands down to the bones and saving up money so I could buy this place. No one thought I could do it. But I just kept my mouth shut and my eyes open because that's what my mama taught me to do. There isn't a square inch of this place that hasn't been touched with these two hands. This place is my baby, my husband, and my destiny all rolled into one. It's all I want, and it's all I need. I rent five rooms out to women, and only women. You must be single, you must have a job, and you must respect my rules. You with me so far?"

"Yes, ma'am."

"So are you married?" The woman looked at Ellie's hand in search of a ring.

Ellie hesitated and sipped her coffee. "No."

Betty noted the pause. "Do you have a job?"

"Not yet. I just got into town today. I plan to look for one tomorrow."

"How you gonna rent a room without a job?"

"My hus—my father gave me some money until I could find something." Ellie pulled the bills from her pocket for proof. "I can pay for the first few nights, and in just a few days I should have a job."

"Who sent you here?"

"I found your ad posted at the train station."

"Train station? Where you comin' from?"

Ellie wasn't sure why she trusted this Betty Bethea, but she did. "Charleston."

"Charleston," Betty repeated, and tilted her head to survey Ellie. She imagined what Betty must think of her appearance—her neat, light-brown hair curled just below the chin; her faded lipstick that left a hint of a color like bougainvilleas. Her inadequate jacket was navy blue, and she knew the outfit looked expensive simply judging by the tightly sewn buttons. Her tan patent leather shoes were barely scuffed.

"Charleston," Betty said again suspiciously. "And you came to Florence on a train." She rocked back and forth and scanned the street. "Where's your luggage?"

"Don't have any."

"Where's your purse? I don't know any white woman don't carry a purse."

"Well, now you do. I don't carry a purse."

"Who you here to see?"

"No one, really. I just wanted to get away for a while. Try someplace different, and this was the first stop off the train." Ellie knew she was saying more than she should, but this woman's demeanor demanded respect and at least a little honesty.

"How do you know you wanna stay here? You haven't even seen the rooms."

"You haven't offered to show me the rooms." Ellie sucked in her breath, realizing she may have been too cheeky.

"Hmm. Backbone. I like that. Come on. I'll show you the room. I only have one left."

Ellie followed Betty up the stairs while Betty presented the house rules.

"Like I said, Backbone, no men allowed. That includes boyfriends, boy dogs, boy cats. I'm not runnin' a brothel here. If you wanna cavort and cohort, then you can find yourself somewhere else to do it. If I so much as smell a man in this house, you're out. Understand?"

"Yes, ma'am."

"You will keep a clean room and you will make your bed daily. I'm not your mama and I am not your maid. When you finish eating in the kitchen, clean your own dishes. This isn't a diner. I don't work for you. I'm doing you a favor by letting you live in my house for a small fee. You are not doing me any favors by being here. I got women comin' by every day lookin' for a clean, safe place to live. Understand, Backbone?" She didn't wait for Ellie to reply. "Fix your own food. Buy your own groceries. Put your name on your groceries so there's no confusion with the other renters. Wash your own clothes. Don't come in past 10:00 p.m. because, trust me, you do not want to disturb my beauty sleep. Do not lock your room door. You shouldn't have anything to hide noways. I won't go in without knocking, so don't worry about that. The other renters have their own money and their own things, and they ain't wantin' yours. So no locks. I think that just about covers it. Wait, and if your rent is so much as one day late, I will knock on your door, enter your room and pack your bags for you. Because I'm nice like that."

She opened the door at the end of the hall and stepped inside. The walls were warm, the color of red wine, and the crown molding was crisp and white. Betty pulled the cord to open the heavy navy blue curtains swirled with a golden stitch of floral embroidery. They swept the glossy hardwood floor as they opened to the gray light that spilled into the room. An oak tree bustled its bare branches outside the window. Betty turned on a lamp on a writing desk in the corner.

"This is the Hughes Room, after my favorite poet, Langston Hughes. Ever heard of him?" Betty asked.

"Sounds familiar," Ellie admitted, "but I can't remember exactly."

"Too much to name, but my favorite is this one." Betty pointed to a picture framed over the writing desk, and Ellie walked over to it. A river had been painted alongside the words.

"What a beautiful painting," Ellie said before even reading the poem. She traced the river lightly with her fingertip over the glass.

"Thank you. It's not nearly as good as the poem, though." Betty's voice sounded softer now.

Ellie read the poem aloud,

"I've known rivers:
I've known rivers ancient as the world and older than the
Flow of human blood in human veins.
My soul has grown deep like the rivers.
I bathed in the Euphrates when dawns were young.
I built my hut near the Congo and it lulled me to sleep.
I looked upon the Nile and raised the pyramids above it.
I heard the singing of the Mississippi when Abe Lincoln went
down to New Orleans,
And I've seen its muddy bosom all golden in the sunset.
I've known rivers:
Ancient, dusky rivers.
My soul has grown deep like the rivers.

You're right," Ellie said. "It is beautiful." She meant it.

"Backbone, let's get to the point. I'm not stupid." Betty stepped closer to Ellie and looked straight into her eyes. "I don't know what river you've been ridin' or where it's been goin' or how long you've been on it, but I know you're trying to climb ashore. And I don't know what your situation is and you don't have to tell me, but I do know that a young girl, eighteen or not, don't just hop off a train and come wanderin' into a strange town one day lookin' for a room to rent. No job. No family here. No friends here. No business here. But it takes a backbone to do it. I have one, too, and I'm tellin' you now, it's the only way to survive." She extended her hand out to Ellie. "You're welcome here, Eleanor McCollum, or whoever you are, and you'll be safe here. Just mind the rules," she smiled.

Chapter Thirteen

The mighty train lay silent now,
Its wheels stricken, bound.
The tracks were bent and mangled there,
The whistle made no sound.
So this is how my journey ends?
So this is all there is?
The devil laughed, the angels gasped,
Christ rose to answer this.

Inside Baker Sanatorium, gurneys lined the hallways with the injured and the deceased, and each hospital room was well past its maximum occupancy. Dr. Baker, the chief surgeon, founder, and owner of the hospital, rushed from patient to patient, stabilizing those who had a chance at life and making comfortable those who didn't. His fellow doctors and nurses were scarce; most had been sent to aid at the war front. He knew his son, a medical student at Duke University, would soon be home to help.

"We need more blood!" Dr. Baker called to an overwhelmed nurse. He was bent over a woman pleading for her foot to be saved.

The woman grabbed his white coat that was smeared with blood. "You have to help me! Please! I have to get to New York City. I have a fashion show to stage, and Sinatra's singing. I have to be there. Please help me!" Panic shot from her eyes like lightning.

"We're going to save your foot," he calmed her. "You'll see Sinatra. And I want a ticket, too, okay?" He smiled to console her and she laid her head back down, unconvinced. The doctor moved the sheet up to the woman's knee to expose the maimed foot and ankle. He could see the bone beneath the flesh; it looked like it had been chewed by a wild animal.

"There is no more blood, Doctor. And we're almost out of sulfa," the nurse informed him.

"Get the Red Cross over here."

"They're nowhere near here. They've mostly been sent to the front as well, and those that are still stateside have empty banks. There's a massive shortage. Can you use mine?" She held out her arm.

Dr. Baker instructed her to call any volunteers she could think of that would be willing to donate blood. Soon, local Robesonians were lined up at the door to offer blood and help in any way they could, including inviting the survivors with minimal injuries into their homes to help them try to contact family members, make transportation arrangements, or just to feed them and keep them warm.

As spaces became available and injured victims were moved to other hospitals, the deceased were being taken to the Red Springs Funeral Home. Heavyheartedly, the military prepared to ship back home the dead bodies that they were able to identify. Lists of the disaster victims' names were checked and updated every hour, many switching columns from injured to dead as the hours wore on. The lists were posted at the front doors of each hospital and funeral home to help ease the indoor congestion of the media and those searching for family members.

Christopher Vaillant read the list posted at the Red Springs Funeral Home. He followed the names line by line and checked twice more when he could not find Eleanor McCollum Vaillant. It frustrated him that the names were not organized in alphabetical order.

"Who are you looking for?" an elderly man asked him. His brown coat was pulled up at the collar, and his black rimmed glasses fell below the bridge of his nose.

"My wife," Christopher answered coldly.

"Me too," the old man's voice cracked. He reached in his pocket for his wrinkled handkerchief and brought it to his mouth. "Her name is Evelyn. She's right there, eighth line down."

Christopher followed down to the eighth line. *Evelyn Douglas, deceased.*

"I'm sorry, sir," Christopher offered.

"Me too. Married for fifty-eight years, we were. She was going to visit her sister in New York." He grabbed onto Christopher's elbow as he tottered, trying to maintain his composure.

"You should probably get yourself home, old man. It's cold out here." He looked around for a bench.

"Home? You want me to go home? What's at home? There's nothing for me there." His head fell to the side to look up at the captain. His eyes were brown and milky and hollow. "Home? It's not home anymore. It's just a house. Just a chair. Just a kitchen. Just a bowl and a spoon and a yard with her rose bushes in it." A tear escaped the corner of his eye.

"Sir," Christopher addressed another gentleman who had come to search the list. "Could you please tend to this man? He's very weak and has just learned of his wife's death." The stranger hurried to his side and helped the old man shuffle back to his car.

Christopher caught the attention of a nurse who had come to update the list. She tucked her clipboard under her armpit and reached to untack the paper from the door.

"Excuse me," he asserted. "I am looking for my wife; she's not on this list. Is there anywhere else she would be? I was directed here."

"Try Baker's," she answered without looking at him. Her hair was disheveled and her voice exhausted. "It's about ten miles east of here." She scribbled a few names and marked a few off, then reclassified some from injured to deceased. Then she retacked it to the door and went back inside.

**

A black Plymouth P11 Business Coupe crawled down the dirt driveway; its fat tires crunched through the iced-over mud puddles in the sandy ruts.

"Doesn't look like anyone's home," agent Donnie Perry said. He followed the bare branches of the pecan tree up into the dismal sky. A dusting of snow held tight to its limbs. "No car in the driveway."

"Maybe they don't own a car," answered Tom Hurley.

"Then why would they have a driveway?"

"This is a farm road, not a driveway. Tractors take this road to the fields. See?" He pointed ahead to the barren field. "But there's smoke coming from the chimney."

Perry looked up at the roof, its brick chimney crooked and sloped to the side, and he saw a thin wire of smoke rising and a hole in the roof.

"Say they call him Pecan. Got a wife, two kids, and a crippled parent living with him." Tom Hurley shifted the gear into park with a clunk.

"What about that dog?" The dog was standing alert with his tail up and his teeth bared.

"They didn't teach you how to handle dogs in the FBI?"

The two men stepped out of the car and ignored the snarling dog who had not yet taken to barking. He trotted to the car and sniffed around the tires, then followed the footsteps of the strangers as they ascended the front steps. They knocked on the wooden screen door that needed repainting.

Pecan Locklear opened the door.

"Good afternoon, sir. I'm Tom Hurley. I'm with the Interstate Commerce Commission, and this is FBI agent Donnie Perry. We need to ask you a few questions about last night's incident, if you don't mind." Perry displayed his badge.

"Come in," Pecan held the screen door open for them. "It's okay, boy," he said to the dog. "You can relax. You've had a long night too." He gave him a rub on his head and smoothed down his ears. His tone and touch assured the dog, so he turned around and settled himself back down on the porch.

Pecan offered the gentlemen a seat at the kitchen table. "Coffee?"

"No, thank you." Perry looked around at the scant rations in the kitchen and didn't believe this family had much coffee to spare. Pecan poured himself a cup.

"We've been told by a few eyewitnesses that you were the first one on the scene," Hurley stated.

"That could be right."

The two men looked at each other. "You aren't sure?"

"I didn't notice. I heard the explosion and went to it."

"Tell us exactly what you saw upon your arrival. Did you walk there?"

"No, sir. I ran. I heard the wreck when it happened, saw fires across those fields and through them trees, and I took to runnin'. When I got there, the fumes were burnin' my eyes and my nose. I seen people strewn around every which way I turned. Some were crawlin' on their knees and some on their bellies, some were tryin' to stand up but didn't have both legs to stand on, and they didn't know it. Some of 'em were just plain still. I heard people screamin' and carryin' on, bangin' from the inside of the train to get out." Pecan rubbed his forehead at the images that were still too fresh to be memories. "People cryin'. Howlin'. Worst sounds I ever heard in my life. I don't ever want to hear 'em again, but I'm afraid I'm gonna keep hearin' 'em for a long, long time." He dropped his eyes and took a sip of his coffee.

"I'm sure it was a gruesome scene. I'm sorry you had to see that. And I hate that we're having to rehash it so soon, but we're just trying to investigate the cause of it."

"I understand."

"Did you hear anything before the crash?"

"Just my dog out there barkin'. He started barkin' thirty minutes or so before the wreck ever happened. I don't know what he was thinkin'."

"That was about the time the first train derailed. He must've heard that. It was a miracle that almost all of those passengers weren't hurt. Only one life lost on the southbound, a Harvard preacher, they said.

They were evacuated out of the cars that fell across the other tracks and built fires while the crew started repairs. Did you see those fires? Did you hear the derailment?"

"No, sir."

"Were you asleep at the time?"

"No, sir. I don't sleep much anymore. I don't know why I didn't hear the derailment. Maybe it wasn't that loud. Maybe I was just thinkin' about somethin' else."

"But you heard your dog."

"After a while, I went out to see what he was so up in arms about. He ain't usually like that. He's a good boy. I didn't see anything but a black night, and I didn't hear anythin' but sleet hittin' the roof."

"Did you hear any aircraft flying overhead before the crash?"

"Aircraft? At that time of night?"

"Some theories hold that a bomb was dropped on the train."

"I thought that too at first until I got there. But that doesn't make any sense. Train would've been blown to bits, not crumpled up like a tin can. And then there'd've been a big hole in the ground, and the rest of the train would've been blown off the tracks, and then no one would be alive, from either train."

"I think you're probably right, Mr. Locklear," Perry said. "But we just have to eliminate all possibilities."

"Well you can eliminate that one."

"Have you seen any suspicious activity in the past few days? Any people hanging around the tracks that aren't usually there? Any kids playing on the tracks? Were your kids playing on the tracks?"

"My kids are not allowed to play on those tracks, and they mind real good. My wife sees to that. And there ain't no reason at all for anyone to need to walk on those tracks. Not way out here."

The two men looked at each other again, satisfied with their questions and their subject's answers.

"As of now," Hurley explained, "it looks like it was a combination of a broken rail, leaking brakes, broken couplings, and the hand of God. Do you have any questions for us, Mr. Locklear?"

A baby cried in the next room.

"I do. What am I supposed to do about that? He's an orphan," Pecan said quietly. "Brought him home from the train wreck."

"Where is his mother?"

"Dead. I pried him from her arms. Father dead too. He was right next to 'em. We ain't real sure what to do. We hope the baby has some kinfolk that can raise him right, but it was too cold out there to sit around and wait for a bunch of briefcases to make the decision. So I brought him home. My wife's been takin' care of him."

"Why haven't you taken him in to the authorities yet?"

"Well I figured the authorities were a little wrapped up last night with other things and he'd be safer here for the night, away from the noise and out of the cold. He's been through enough. And this morning I didn't quite have it in me to walk ten miles to the nearest hospital. Besides, all of our blankets were at the wreck. I've got nothin' to wrap him up in."

Hurley nodded. "I'll let the authorities know about the baby, and they'll send someone out to get him. Did you happen to grab anything that may help to identify his family? A purse or a scarf or anything that was in the vicinity of his mother?"

"No, sir. That thought would've been the last thing to cross my mind at the time. I just needed to get that baby safe. That's all."

"Of course. Well it's very kind of you and your wife to take care of him. Or," he looked at Perry, "would you prefer that we take him with us now?"

Perry shot him a wide-eyed glare. "I don't know anything about taking care of babies."

"For crying out loud, Donnie, you have four kids at home."

"I just make the money to feed them. I let the wife handle the rest of it."

Hurley shook his head. "I'm no expert either, but if the baby is a burden to you and your family, Mr. Locklear, I'm sure that we can figure out how to expediently get him to safekeeping."

"There is no such thing as a baby bein' a burden. We'll just keep him here until y'all figure somethin' out. He'll be safe here. Miranda's real good with babies."

"I don't doubt that," Hurley said and stood from his chair. He grabbed his hat, fit it down on his head, and extended his hand to Pecan.

"Thank you for everything, Mr. Locklear. The families of the victims owe a great deal of gratitude to you, and you're a saint to keep a baby that isn't even yours."

"Well, I 'preciate that. But I didn't do anything that anyone else wouldn't have done. That's what we're here for, right? Gotta help each other when we can."

Something under the candle on the table caught Perry's eye.

"Is that why you can't sleep?" Perry asked Pecan. Pecan turned to look and saw Perry's gaze fastened on the piece of paper.

"May I?"

Pecan nodded while Perry reached for the paper. "How long ago did you get this?"

"A couple weeks."

"What are you going to do?"

"Do I have a choice? Says I've been drafted. Doesn't ask me whether I want to be or not."

"Don't you want to fight for your country?" Hurley asked.

"I don't agree with war, sir. They don't have anything I want over there in Europe or Germany or Japan or anywhere else they're fightin'. I don't see why we don't just leave 'em alone and protect our own. Too many men as it is over there dyin', and dyin' on someone else's land for somebody else's problems. Now, they want me to go over and die on somebody else's land. It don't make sense to me. If I'm standin' in front of my own tree, I'll fight for my tree. But I don't want to go all the way across the ocean to fight for someone else's tree that ain't got nothin' to do with me. I have a family here that needs me. If I go, what'll my wife do? How'll my kids eat? My dad can't work on account of his bad leg, and my wife can't work 'cause she's got the youngins. It's up to me to take care of my family, and how am I gonna do that if I'm not here?"

Perry considered Pecan's conflict.

"You understand, though," Hurley challenged, "that the Nazis are decimating an entire population of people solely based on their race? You get that, right? That he's invading countries that don't belong to him and taking them?"

"With all due respect, sir, I understand that far more than you ever will," Pecan answered quietly.

"Without us, without the United States," Hurley ignored Pecan's comment, "Hitler will take Europe. They need us. You just said yourself that that's what we're supposed to do—help each other."

"War won't never be all the way right or all the way wrong," Pecan said. "Sir, I'm Native American. If we'd fought for our land and for our own trees the first time around, things may be different now. But we didn't fight for it. Or, maybe we didn't fight hard enough. Either way, war or not, here we are. And I heard you said earlier that God's hand had a part in the train wreck. God didn't cause that wreck. People caused it. God don't make bad things happen. He allows 'em to happen, and He allows 'em to happen because we ain't machines. We make our own choices, and I feel like we break His heart every day with our choices. War is one of those choices. If I could, I'd choose not to fight. You choose to fight. That doesn't make me good or you bad or you good and me bad. That just makes us not machines."

Miranda leaned against the doorway with her arms crossed, listening.

"Yet our soldiers are over there dying every day so you can sit here and enjoy your free choices. You want someone else to slaughter the bull, but you want to eat the meat. Is that it?" Hurley's face was reddening.

"I have my own bull to slaughter. Do I have to wear a helmet and shoot a gun to help my country? Is that the only way? Some men need to hold a gun, and so they should. I respect that, and I am thankful. But if I had been holding a gun last night, if I had been at war, I wouldn't have been here to hear that train. I wouldn't have been here to help those wounded soldiers. I wouldn't have been here to keep that old lady warm with my grandmother's quilt. I wouldn't have been able to give some of them people a warm drink and a blanket and some hopeful words. And I wouldn't have been here to get to that baby. And the doctors that fought all night to save them, they didn't fight with guns. The nurses and the neighbors that all came together to help these poor people—they didn't need to fight far away to help their country. They fought right here for their own trees in their own yards. It's still war, but if we're all standin' in the same place, then only that place gets saved. People have diff'rent kinds of wars, and there are diff'rent ways to fight 'em. My war is tryin' to figure out how to keep my kids fed."

"With all due respect to your personal struggles, it just seems to me that getting your brains blown out at point blank range or not knowing if you're going to come home again or being captured and tortured by the enemy is a smidge more painful, a little harder," Hurley recanted.

"It's just a different kind of pain, sir. That's all. But one of 'em lasts a lot longer."

Hurley shifted uncomfortably, and the three men stood silently, considering. Manny Locklear was standing in the doorway and interrupted them.

"I didn't know, son," he said.

"I didn't tell you."

"I'll help out however I can."

"I can help too," said Perry. "Hand it to me," he held out his palm. Pecan passed the paper.

"I'll see to it that you're waived from the draft order." Perry folded the paper and tucked it inside his coat pocket. "It was a pleasure to meet you and your family, Mr. Locklear." He touched the rim of his hat and gave a respectful nod to Miranda and Manny, then he shook Pecan's hand.

"We'll send word about the baby," Hurley said curtly.

"Thank you," Pecan replied. "I 'preciate that."

The men started down the porch steps. The dog came out from under the porch again and growled as he followed behind them to the car.

"He sure doesn't like you," Perry joked to Hurley.

"Well I don't much like him either," Hurley huffed. "Why are you helping him out of the draft anyway?"

"I was talking about the dog."

**

Captain Vaillant studied the road map as he and the private drove away from the sanatorium. The dark red bricks and white shutters soon faded from view while his frustration rose like the tide. He had examined the list of names posted; he even carefully deciphered the original names beneath those that had been scratched through. His wife's was not among them either. He asked several nurses and staff members and patients at the hospital if they had seen her. "Chin-length brown hair," he told them. "Medium height. Slim build. Named Eleanor Vaillant." No one recalled.

"You've just physically described ninety percent of the female population, Captain," one nurse told him.

"She wasn't on that train when it crashed, Private," Christopher said when he climbed back into the military jeep.

"But, sir, you found her purse."

"I found her purse with her wedding ring in it and the money gone. If she'd been on that train, the money would've still been in her purse, and that ring would've been on her finger. So there's only one other place she could be, Private: Florence, South Carolina. It's the only train stop between Fayetteville and Charleston. She won't be hard to find there."

"What if she returned to Charleston, sir?"

"She wouldn't do that just yet. I think she has a bee in her bonnet now that she thinks she's grown. We'll find her, Private," he said confidently. "She's getting ready to find out that bee's going to sting a bit."

The private said nothing and followed the captain's directions. He checked his watch.

"We don't have much time. I'm scheduled to depart at midnight. Speed this clunker up a bit." The jeep jolted with the accelerator.

Nearly two hours later, they pulled into the train depot in Florence, South Carolina. Christopher climbed out of the jeep and straightened his uniform.

"Stand by, Private."

He opened the heavy doors of the depot and approached the ticket booth. The floors were polished marble, and most of the benches were empty.

"Excuse me, sir," he addressed the agent. "My name is Captain Christopher Vaillant, US Army. I am looking for a particular civilian and am hoping you can help me."

"Yes, sir, I can try," the young man said. He sat up a little straighter to show respect to the distinguished soldier before him and he pushed his glasses back up his nose.

"I'm looking for a young woman, some might describe her as rather plain, light-brown hair, chin-length, stands about five foot four inches, and she would have been debarking here yesterday late afternoon."

"Well, sir, we have lots of women coming through here, and I can't say that I would have recognized the woman you're looking for. Which train was she coming in on?" He shuffled his papers to find the itinerary.

"Tamiami Champion Number Eight."

The ticket agent froze. "Sir," he said slowly. "You realize that's the train that ..."

"Yes, it crashed. I'm aware. But my wife wasn't on it. I think she got off here, before it crashed."

"Whoa! That was a piece of luck, wasn't it?" he brightened. "Can you imagine if she hadn't gotten off that train? I hear it's a grisly scene up there. Just awful. All those people, just trying to get home for the holidays. And those trains just went pow!" He simulated an explosion with his hands. "I think that's why no one's hardly here today. They're all too scared to get on a train." His eyes were wide and he nodded, hoping for a reward for his keen observation.

"The tracks are fouled, nitwit. All trains have been canceled until they clear the wreckage. Shouldn't you already know that?" He was irritated.

The young man checked the itinerary again nervously.

"So you don't recall anyone by that description?" Christopher reminded him of his purpose.

"No, sir, I'm sorry. I don't."

"Last question, not that I expect you to know much more than where your pants are every morning. Are there any homes for women nearby, or any affordable hotels, so to speak, for a gal just arriving into town with nowhere to stay?"

"There are several listed on the community board over there, sir." He pointed to a corkboard overrun with flyers and slips of paper tacked to it.

He checked his watch. He estimated it would take another four hours to get to Fort Moultrie.

Shuffling through the scraps pinned to the cork, something caught his eye: *McKeller House. Rooms to let. 208 Ranier Street. Women only.* He returned to the agent with the ad in his hand.

"Where is Ranier Street?"

"Just a few blocks that way," he answered. He pointed behind his head to the southwest corner of the depot.

The young man half saluted him as he rushed away.

In minutes the jeep pulled alongside the manicured curb of the large blue house.

"This is the place," he confirmed.

Christopher dusted off his hat and pushed it back down onto his head. He straightened his tie and smoothed his coat and wiped the ashen mud that was stuck to the sides of his shoes. She had to be here. He surveyed the azalea bushes that lined the home's foundation and counted the windows along the front. Four big windows and a formidable front door. The second floor had five windows, and he stared at each one of them, imagining which one Ellie was behind. She had to be here.

He thumbed the ring on his pinkie. *Why would she have taken this off?* he wondered. *Why would she be hiding from me? I was giving her a new life. A new home. We were going to start our family. Maybe it's a simple explanation. Maybe she had a premonition about the train, or maybe she was feeling sick and needed to stop off for the night—could she have morning sickness so soon?*

Suddenly a curtain moved, and he thought he caught a glimpse of Ellie's face. He marched up the steps, determined to retrieve his bride, and rang the buzzer.

**

Betty Bethea had seen him coming through the kitchen window. She was wiping down the red-and-white gingham tablecloth when she saw the military jeep pull up.

"Now what in this round world is this man wantin' from here?" she mumbled to herself and slung the dishrag over her shoulder. She opened the big door but left the screened door latched. "Yes? Can I help you?"

"I hope so. I am here to see Eleanor Vaillant." Christopher removed his hat.

"What's that name again?" she stalled. She wasn't sure how to respond. Was this someone Eleanor wanted to see? He was handsome, and he was an officer. He was also wearing a wedding band. But the last name was wrong. Or could this be why she was hiding?

"Vaillant. Eleanor Vaillant." Christopher recognized her hesitancy. "I see you recognize the name; that's great. It's okay. She should be expecting me." He bore his eyes into hers to gauge her reaction.

"Well, I'm sorry but that name actually doesn't ring a bell."

"I see. I'd like to speak to the owner of the home then. Perhaps she could be of more assistance to me."

"Of course, sir. Just one moment." Betty shut the door, counted to three, and reopened the door. "Hello. How can I help you?" She cocked her head and smirked.

"Ah. My apologies. You own this whole place?" He waved his arm to encompass the porch.

"Every inch of it."

"I see. Well, that's very good. Good for you. I didn't catch your name?"

"That's because I didn't tell you my name."

"Here it is," he pulled out the scrap of paper. "Betty Bethea, is it?" She did not answer him.

"You see, this is very important, and I haven't a lot of time. Eleanor Vaillant is my wife, and she was supposed to have arrived in Fayetteville, North Carolina, very early this morning. However, you may have heard that the very train she was on was involved in a collision. There were many, many fatalities. As you can imagine, I've been searching everywhere for her. I searched the wreckage and found some of her things, and then I checked the lists of passengers accounted for at all the hospitals and morgues. I have since come to believe that she was not on that train at all. It's a miracle, really, that she wasn't. I don't know how I could have lived had she been killed on that train. Especially since she was coming to see me—we're newlyweds, you understand—and to move in to our new home." He held his hat to his heart for emphasis. "Now, I have learned that she is here. It's such a relief. I've come a long way, Miss Bethea, and I'm here to take my bride home. Please, tell her that her husband is here. Tell her she's safe now." He softened his voice and smiled.

Betty was unimpressed by his performance.

"While that is a touching story, sir, I don't know anyone by that name. Maybe you should look elsewhere."

"But she is here."

"She is not here."

"Miss Bethea, as I stated earlier, I don't have a lot of time. Please, tell her I am here."

"Mr. Officer, as I have stated, there is no one here by that name." She convinced herself that since Eleanor had not said the name "Vaillant," she was not lying to a ranked official of the United States government.

"Very well, I will wait until she returns." The captain returned his hat to his head and straightened his shoulders. He turned to walk to the rocking chairs.

"Sir, you are most welcome to wait for a very short time. Past that, you are trespassing. You see, those rockers are reserved for my guests. You are not a guest. You may not sit in them."

He paused. "Shall I assume, Miss Bethea, that you have all of the proper licensure to both own this property and conduct a business here?" He tilted his head and inspected the light blue porch ceiling. "Is that a leak there? And your codes, are they filed and up to standards? Taxes current? I'm sure you've been audited, yes?"

He drew his eyes slowly back to her, arrested by the haughty poise of her chin.

"Yes. You shall assume." She shut the front door and locked it. Her heart was pounding.

Now what? she wondered. This man was a menace. He stood just outside the front door, close enough that the screen door would hit him if it opened. He stared straight ahead through the glass, his stance like a soldier in a company lineup. He fixed his eyes on the staircase. From there he could see any activity coming or going from and within the house.

Betty began to doubt herself. She couldn't jeopardize her livelihood. She'd worked too hard and too long and fought too many battles to have it taken away from her now, especially for the sake of a secretive stranger. Maybe she should just go get Eleanor and be done with this. She could tell the captain that she was here and explain the misunderstanding of the last name. Then he would leave Florence and leave her alone and this would all go away.

Why did she feel compelled to help this girl? She thought of the other staircase, the servants' staircase that went from the kitchen to the upstairs at the back of the house. No, she wouldn't. She refused to go that way. That staircase was haunted, she reminded herself. Too many times she had felt something there when she was first renovating the steps. The boards were rotted with age, and every time Betty tore up a plank and nailed a new one down, she thought she felt a hand on her shoulder. The first few times she hoped it was her imagination. She tried to reason that it was just her sweat making her shirt stick to her. Or that it was her muscle having spasms from the hammering. But it kept happening, and when a cool wisp of air drifted across her neck at the same time that a hand rested on her shoulder, she stopped trying to explain it. Instead, she backed down the stairwell as quickly as she could, and then she slid a giant cupboard in front of the staircase to block it. She didn't deal with spirits, no sir. A shiver crawled up her spine and she shook it away. She would not go up those stairs.

The captain remained standing at the front door while Betty walked to the kitchen. She grabbed the dishrag from her shoulder and snapped at a fly on the counter. She grabbed a clean rag and started drying dishes to busy herself. But the man on her porch gave her an uneasy feeling. There was something sinister about him, she thought. A malicious motive behind a handsome face. A messy soul cloaked by a clean, smart uniform. And Eleanor was so young. So naive. Too stupid to see it.

No, not too stupid to see it, Betty realized. That's why she's here. That's why she got off the train.

"Lord knows, I know what that feels like," Betty said aloud. She lined her back and rear end up against the side of the cupboard and pushed it slowly so it wouldn't scrub the floor with too much noise. The dishes inside clinked and rattled with the movement.

She took a deep breath and stared up into the dark staircase. She couldn't remember which steps were missing, and she had never replaced the flickering light bulb that hung from an electrical wire.

No, she couldn't do it.

She had to. She had to warn Ellie.

The staircase was too narrow for a banister, so she clung to the wall as she ascended. She could feel the gouges where the chunks of plaster had crumbled away from the wall. She reached her toes out to feel for each plank before stepping and then remembered that there were two consecutive missing steps. She would have to jump to reach the next step. No, she would crawl, she decided. The stairwell was musty, and her hands on the dusty floor caught cobwebs as she poked around for a flat surface. Then she felt something on her shoulder. Bolting up the remaining stairs, she burst through the door and tumbled out onto the second floor. A young woman stood there staring at her with wide eyes.

"Betty! Are you okay? I thought you were a ghost! You scared me to death!"

"I'm fine, Sara. Just wanted to give the old staircase a try." She stood up and dusted herself off. "Listen, there's a strange man on the front porch. It's not safe for you to go down right now."

"What does he want?" she asked. She clutched at her neckline.

"He's lookin' for someone. None of our business. He'll go away soon enough. Just don't go downstairs right now, okay?"

The young woman returned to her room and shut the door behind her.

"Backbone," Betty whispered through the crack in the door she knocked softly.

"Eleanor!"

Ellie opened the door.

They heard Christopher's voice shouting outside.

"Eleanor Vaillant! I know you're in there! It's me, honey. It's Christopher, your husband. The one you vowed to love till the end of time. Well, it's not the end of time yet, dear."

Ellie and Betty snuck to the window to peek outside. Christopher was standing in the front yard looking up at each of the windows. He didn't see them, but his arms were waving wide.

"Hello! Mrs. Vaillant. Come on down now. It's time to go. I'm sailing for France soon, and you need to see me off like a proper wife. There's this thing called the war, remember? Men get killed. I just want to see your face before I go. Ellie," he lilted. "My Ellie, my wife."

Ellie started shaking and looked at Betty like a mouse under a hawk's shadow.

"I didn't tell him you were here," Betty told her. "I said there was no one here by that name. He doesn't believe me."

"How in the world did he find me here? I have to hide, Betty. What do I do?"

"First of all, he can't come inside. The doors are all locked. Now you need to get to tellin' the truth so I'll know exactly what I'm dealin' with here. What did you drag to my house?"

"He …" Ellie stuttered. "He's my husband. We were married two days ago, and I realized he's an awful person. I didn't know what else to do, so I left everything on the train." She was ashamed to say it out loud. "I thought it would be months before he came home and realized I'd left him. He's supposed to be leaving for the war today. I don't know why he's here. I don't know how he found me."

"It's okay, Ellie," Christopher continued shouting from the yard. "I know you took off your wedding ring. I don't know why," he laughed basely, "but I'm running out of time, and I need to get back to Moultrie. Listen, we can talk about all of that on our way back down, and I'll buy you another train ticket and we can try this again. I'm giving you another chance, Eleanor, because I love you."

"He's not going to go away without me," she told Betty. "He isn't accustomed to losing. Not at anything. I have to go down."

The private stepped out of the jeep. "Sir, it's time. We need to be leaving now."

At this the captain yelled louder, "You hear that, Eleanor Vaillant? I have to leave now! I have to go to war and fight for people like you that like to hide in corners and pretend that things don't exist. I have to go and hope to not die, for people like you who don't keep their promises and don't appreciate the things that have been given to you by people like me. But I'm going to leave you with this …." He opened the jeep door and pulled out a purse from the floorboard. "I'm going to leave your purse here for you. I found it in the wreckage, you see." He held it up high to the windows. "And I put your wedding ring back in the pocket where I found it. We'll sort that out later. So come on down here and get your purse. I put a little more money in it for you, since you've obviously already spent what I left you. And your house key is here; everything is here. Everything you wanted to start our life together is in here." He laid the purse gently in the grass on the lawn and slowly backed away from it, his hands held up and his palms exposed. He leaned against the jeep and waited.

"No," Betty said quietly. She understood now. "You don't have to do that. You don't have to have that life." She placed her hand on Ellie's. "I didn't."

Ellie squeezed Betty's hand. "That's what rivers are for then, aren't they?" Ellie looked back at the poem on the wall. "For moving along. For not having to stay in the same place."

"'My soul has grown deep like the rivers,'" Betty whispered it like a prayer.

They heard the jeep crank up, and they peeked through the crack in the curtain.

"If you aren't home when I get back, Mrs. Vaillant, if I make it back, then I'll come find you," Christopher yelled above the raspy engine. "I'll find you and take you home. With me. You're mine, my love. Mine."

Chapter Fourteen

"Yes, truly, My loves, truly, dears,
This is where it ends.
It's time to board a different train
Your destination now depends:
Did you love your fellow man
And love Me just the same?
Or did you squander gifted time
By praising flesh and gain?
Did you forgive a neighbor's wrong
And help him lift his stone?
If you had kindness, faith, and love,
Then welcome. Welcome home."

Dr. Jackson had been awake for over thirty-six hours straight. He had changed his white coat several times now, but it was once again smeared with dirt and blood and other excretions. His back ached as he leaned over another patient.

"Looks like maybe you were the one in the train wreck, Doc," the soldier said, as he shifted his weight on the gurney. Sharp pains darted across his torso, and he grimaced. The doctor urged him to put his head back down on the wadded-up jacket being used as a makeshift pillow.

"Probably does," he smiled weakly. "But I think you have the honors on that one, soldier. You've been unconscious for almost two days. Glad you decided to join us." The doctor lifted the edges of the bandage on the soldier's head. The gauze was sticky with the coagulated blood. "Had a pretty deep gash on your brow here. Could probably use some stitches, but I wanted to wait to see the whites of your eyes before I stitched you up."

"You mean you wanted to wait to see if I was going to pull through?"

"Precisely." The doctor made no apologies.

"Well, here I am. But I'm not sure why. How many dead, Doc?"

"We're still counting. Right now we're up to sixty-eight."

The soldier said nothing. He shifted his eyes to the ceiling.

"You have four broken ribs, but there's really nothing we can do for that. We've got you wrapped up, but it's going to take some time for those to heal. I don't suppose I need to tell you to lay off any manual labor or heavy lifting. You won't be returning to service anytime soon, I'm sorry to say. But you're lucky to be alive, son. I didn't catch your name."

"Merritt. James Merritt."

"Well, James Merritt, you're a lucky man." Dr. Jackson held the clipboard up close to his eyes. "Says here you were pulled out of the first car that collided with the train. Not sure how it is that you're still with us, young man. Nurse," he addressed Sadie Currie. "We need these bandages removed. Clean the area and prepare him for stitches. I'll be back as soon as I can to sew him up." He moved on to the next patient in the room.

Sadie clicked on her crutches as she made her way to a bowl of water sitting on a table by the gurney. She dipped a rag in the tin bowl and twisted the excess out. She unwrapped the bandage from the patient's head and dabbed the wet rag to soften the dried blood.

"What happened to your foot?"

"Oh, just slipped on some ice at the wreck. Broke my ankle," she said nonchalantly.

"You were there?"

"I was." She rinsed the rag and squeezed it out again.

"Me too."

She smiled. "I might have guessed as much. Either that, or you smarted off to your wife and she clubbed you over the head with a cast iron skillet."

"That would've been better, I think. But I don't have a wife." A snapshot of Meredith flashed in his mind.

"Sure you do."

"No, I don't."

"You just don't remember that you do. You took a pretty strong hit to the head."

"I wouldn't forget having a wife."

"And yet you did."

"What do you mean?"

"I mean she's here." Sadie applied the rag directly to the wound's opening, and James let out a cry. "Shhh," she quieted him. "Toughen up, soldier. It's just a scrape." She smiled to let him know she was teasing him.

"Ma'am, you must be mistaken. I'm not married."

"Quit arguing with me or I'm going to be the one to hit you over the head with a skillet!"

The doctor returned with a small metal tray of surgical supplies.

"Doctor Jackson," Sadie turned him to the side and spoke low into his ear. "I believe he may be experiencing some slight amnesia. He doesn't remember his wife, or even that he is married at all."

The doctor nodded in understanding and snapped on his surgical gloves. He leaned in to lift James's eyelids and shined a tiny light into his pupils. "Mr. Merritt, I'm going to ask you a few questions before I stitch you up, okay?"

It reminded James of the light he saw at the train just before the crew pulled him out. "Sure."

"What is your full name?"

"James Merritt."

"No middle name?"

"David."

"Where do you live?"

"Wherever the army tells me to live." The doctor shot a concerned glance at the nurse.

"Then where are you from originally? Where is your family from?"

"Ridgeland, New Jersey. That's where my folks live. I grew up there."

"Is that where you were headed on the train? Home?"

The question struck him like a tire iron to the kidney. He paused to think about his answer. Where was he going? And most of all, why was he going? What had he been thinking? *It was an asinine assumption*, he chided himself. He didn't have a home, and there was nowhere for him to go. He didn't have anyone waiting for him at the end of the line or anywhere in between. Nor should he expect to. He was the one who left home. He left his parents without explanation or goodbye. He left Meredith behind to bear the brunt of his recklessness. He left his comrades under a tarp on the other side of the ocean. He was the worst kind of coward. And he expected to just step off a train and waltz back home? To walk back into town and set his suitcase down, say he was sorry, and just pick up where he wished he had left off? *What a fool*, he berated himself.

"Bragg," he lied. "I was headed to Fort Bragg."

"Are you married?"

"No." He lowered his eyes.

"Ever been married before? Engaged? Have a sweetheart?"

"No to all of the above."

"I see. All right, Mr. Merritt." The doctor turned to look at the nurse and nodded to credit to her suspicions. "This will be very uncomfortable, Mr. Merritt, but you've probably endured worse things on a battlefield, judging by the medal on your coat. Lie back and try to stay still. Nurse, if you'll try to steady his head."

Sadie put one palm on James's hairline and the other on his jaw. "You are one handsome thing," she told him. "You're going to look like Gary Cooper by the time Doc's finished with you."

The doctor wiped the wound with iodine and began to stitch.

"I'm sorry we weren't able to numb you up for this," he tried to keep talking to keep his patient calm and distracted. "We were low on supplies as it was. Most of it went to the front lines, and rightfully so. No one could've predicted a tragedy like this to come on the home front."

But James was thinking of other things. He jerked each time the needle penetrated his flesh; he could feel the tug of the thread sliding through. But he had hurt people far worse than this. He deserved to feel this. Here he was, surviving what should have killed him yet again. He should have died on that train. Better yet, he should've stepped out in front of it when he had the chance in Charleston. Instead he was here, being mended, stitched back together again. The others—Luther and Michael, and so many others out on the fronts and in ditches and in jungles and on the train—couldn't be stitched or mended. They could only be wrapped up in their coffins. His parents would never mend. And Meredith. He may as well have ripped her open with a shard of metal from the annihilated train.

"Just let me die," he whispered. He kept his eyes closed.

"Don't be so dramatic, handsome," the nurse cooed at him. "It's almost over."

He didn't bother to explain.

"All done, soldier. Sadie, if you'll get him cleaned up and show him his uniform, he's free to leave with his family." The doctor turned to shake his hand. "This is something you'll never forget for the rest of your life, young man. I know I won't. Good luck to you."

"Thank you, Doc, but I don't have any family," James mumbled under his breath.

The nurse brought his uniform over to him. It hung from a wire hanger and had been neatly pressed. His medal had been polished and re-pinned, making new holes in the fabric.

"I believe this belongs to you. Some of the local ladies from town volunteered to come in and gather some of the survivors' clothes for laundering. Wasn't that sweet? I believe Ms. Ellen came and got yours. I went to high school with her. She is a hoot if I've ever seen one. Now let's wash that face of yours, and then I'll pull the curtain so you can get dressed and get on your way. Shall I tell your wife to come help you dress? You're going to have a hard time getting your arms in that shirt with those broken ribs."

"Ma'am, please. I've told you. I don't have a wife. Really, I don't." James gasped when he tried to move his legs to the floor.

"Well, whatever you say. But you can hardly stand up by yourself. I'm going to go get whoever it is out there that claims to be your wife. I'd help you myself, but then we'd both be on the floor." The nurse pulled the curtain and hobbled out on her crutches.

James froze in pain and fear. It had to be a case of mistaken identity. He arranged his feet on the floor and grabbed the gurney's side rails to stand. His legs felt good and strong. Breathing would be the worst part. He coughed a little and the sharp pain jolted him. Upright, he reached gingerly for his uniform.

"James?"

Something was familiar in the lilt of this voice.

"James? Are you in there?" It was a low, soft voice. Scared, even.

He didn't want to answer. He looked around for an escape. There was a window, but a hospital bed was just beneath it, and the person lying there turned to look at him. The man's sheets were bloody and tucked under him, outlining a missing arm. His skin was pale, and he didn't seem to have the strength to blink. He stared listlessly at James.

A finger reached into the gap of the drawn white curtain. It was long and clean, and the fingernail was painted pink. The other fingers curled around the curtain and slowly pulled it back.

"Meredith," James whispered when he saw her face. She was beautiful and soft and surreal.

A timorous smile was on her face, and her eyes searched him up and down.

"Hi," she said nervously. "I just came because, well ..." She stumbled over her words. "I didn't know if you needed help or not. Or a ride to somewhere. Or, well, I wasn't even sure if you were, you know, alive."

"I am. I'm alive," he answered. He didn't know how to do this.

"I see that." She smiled again.

Neither dared look away.

"So, do you? Need help? Or a ride or anything?"

"How did you get here? How did you know I was here?" He had so many questions, and he couldn't tear his eyes away from the sight of her standing there.

"Your parents brought me. They're waiting outside ... in the car."

He needed to sit down. He grimaced as he tried to sit, and Meredith rushed forward to grab his elbow to ease him back down onto the edge of the bed. Her hand felt cool on his skin.

"Both of them? Mom and Dad?"

"Yes."

"But how did they know I was here? How did you all even know I was on that train?"

"We didn't know until the army called. Your dad got the call late last night. They told him that you had survived the wreck and you'd been admitted to Baker Sanatorium in Lumberton, North Carolina. He tried to ask if you were okay, or for any details at all, but they wouldn't tell him anything other than that you were alive. So he threw a suitcase in the car, and so here we all are. Can I help you with your slacks?"

"My parents came for me?"

"Yes. We drove all night and we found your name on the roster outside. Your mom cried the whole way here. Then your dad cried when he saw your name."

James's eyes welled with tears. "And you? You came with them?"

"I'm standing here, aren't I?"

"Why?"

"I guess I came because ..." She hesitated. "I guess it's because you never gave me a chance. And I didn't think that was fair."

"No, it wasn't. But I don't know how you could even speak to me after what I did to you."

The nurse interrupted them and pulled the rest of the curtain back with one of her crutches.

"How long does it take a man to put his britches on? Let's go, Gary Cooper. I don't mean to rush you two, but we got other people needing this bed." She grabbed his pants and handed them to Meredith. "Slap those on your handsome hubby here and y'all get on out of here. Y'all are gonna have to goo goo over each other somewhere else." She turned to James. "I told you you had a wife," and she winked at him.

Meredith blushed as she obediently stooped to help James get his feet into his pants and pulled them up for him. She turned her head away when he buttoned and zipped at the waist.

"Oh dear," they heard the nurse say. "Mr. Dugard? Mr. Dugard? Doc!" she called out of the door. "I think we lost one here." She adjusted her crutches and approached the man beneath the window. "Oh dear. He's gone." She felt his neck for a pulse, closed his eyelids, and pulled the sheet over his face.

The doctor came in. "He lost too much blood." He shook his head and checked for a pulse again. "That makes seventy." His voice was grave and tired.

"Young lady," she addressed Meredith. "I hope you know you are one lucky woman. You're not a widow today."

"Let me help you up," Meredith offered, not responding to the nurse's comment about luck. She put James's arm around her shoulders, and she slid her arm around his waist to support him. "Your parents and Ja—. Well, everyone's right outside."

A tall, slender man with a tan trench coat and a brown hat paced back and forth the length of his automobile. His collar was pulled high around his neck, and his peppered hair was cut neat and short at the collar's edge. He had just finished his cigarette and dropped it into the puddle at his feet and heard it hiss. He turned to look at the hospital door and saw his son. He didn't go to him. He didn't smile. He didn't open his arms. He cried. He stood straight up and held his shoulders back and cried. He didn't wipe away the tears that blurred his vision, and he didn't begrudge the warmth that spread inside his chest. He just said, "Son."

Meredith and James drew closer.

"Dad," James said. His father extended his hand for a handshake and they shook.

His father moved to the passenger door and opened it for his wife.

"Mom." James was sobbing now.

She scrambled out of the car, and several wadded tissues fell from her lap.

She put her arms around him and paid no mind to his wincing.

"His ribs are broken," Meredith told her, using her hand to separate them a little.

"Oh my goodness, I'm so sorry! Did I hurt you? Which ones are broken? They didn't fix those in there? What happened to your head? Are you okay?" If all she could grab was his hands, then she would hold them and never let them go again. "You have blisters!" she inspected his fingertips and his palms.

"Let's get this kid home, hon," Mr. Merritt said to his wife. They looked at each nervously as the back seat door was opened for James and Meredith. A baby was asleep on the seat, curled like a cat beneath a blanket.

James froze. He looked at Meredith with terror in his eyes. She nodded. He looked at his mother; she smiled.

"He's a good kid," his father said, and he walked around to the driver's side and cranked the car. "Get in. It's cold out here, and we have a long way to go."

Meredith carefully touched the child's cheek as she sat down, and James maneuvered himself painfully into the back seat with them. The sleeping child's feet shifted and pushed against James's leg. James was scared to touch him.

This was all too much. He could still escape, he thought. He rested his hand on the door handle. *I don't know if I can do this.* Being part of a family was one thing, but being responsible for your own family was entirely another. He didn't know how to be a husband. He didn't know how to be a father. Hell, he was barely even a son.

He looked over at Meredith. Her fingers stroked the child's brown curls, and she was looking out of her window. The car began creeping forward, its tires crunching the gravel below. He gripped the handle tighter. His mother turned around to look at him, and she smiled, still wiping the tears that wouldn't stop coming. His father glanced at him through the rearview mirror, steadfast and calm. And the child—he had never seen anything purer. He ached to put his hand on the blanket, to see if it was all real.

"I named him after you," Meredith said to James. "We call him Jamey."

A boy, he thought. *My boy. James Merritt Jr. Jamey.* Why would she name him after someone who had done her so terribly wrong? He looked at Meredith, wondering if she could read his thoughts.

"I don't know what to do," he blurted out. He squeezed the door handle, and his sharp knuckles looked like they would burst through his skin.

"How could you know what to do?" she answered calmly. "Have you ever been a father before? A husband? Then how could you possibly know what to do?"

James was breathing heavy now; a panic was just one thought away.

"Mr. Merritt," Meredith put her hand on his shoulder. "Would you please pull the car over?"

He did.

She shifted in her seat and turned to face James. The child stirred.

"I didn't know what to do either. You have put me through hell, James Merritt. Utter hell. Do you have any idea what it's like to be thrown out by your own parents because you have a baby in your belly that shouldn't be there? I have lost all of my friends, all of my family, and all of my dignity. My father bought me a house in a different town so that I wouldn't shame the family any more than I already had with my bastard child. He handed me the key and said good luck with your life, that he would not be a part of it." She kept her voice low to not wake the boy. "So don't tell me you don't know what to do. You never even considered what to do. You just ran away. And then you got rewarded for running away," she glanced at the medal pinned to his uniform. "I didn't have the luxury of running away. I bought myself a cheap band from the dime store and pretended that I was married to you so when I went to the store I wouldn't have to feel those awful, judgmental stares anymore. I lied to everyone. I told them we were married. I found a new church and I lied to them too. I told them my husband was away in the war, and I pretended that this was the life we had chosen for ourselves. And I nearly quit pretending because when I thought of you, I got sick to my stomach. I hated you. I almost didn't let this happen." She put her hand on the baby. "Then one day your mother knocked on my door. She brought me a baby blanket that she'd knitted." Meredith paused to collect herself. "She grabbed my hands, and she told me that no matter what, that child would be loved. With or without you, she said, that child would grow up to know what love was and what a home was and what a family was. And I will forever be grateful for what your parents have done for us. So you need to decide right now. Are you going to come with us? Or are you going to run away again? I see your hand on the door. Either open it and go, or lock yourself in and let's get going. I won't stop you either way."

The baby was waking now and squirmed in the seat. Meredith picked him up and held him to her chest. Still groggy, he looked at James. His eyes were big and green and beautiful.

This is the thing he had been waiting for, right? Isn't this what he'd been wanting, this chance at redemption? This chance to make life good again? This was the reason, wasn't it, that he didn't step out in front of the train in Charleston? And yet this was the very thing that his nightmares had been made of. Here it was in front of him, hand extended and waiting for acceptance. His sobbing mother and his disappointed father and his wife that wasn't yet a wife, and could he even love her? And this child. God, help him, this beautiful child.

Another battle in another war, he thought. It was time to raise his rifle and shoot to kill or lay down his arms for good.

"Make your decision, James," she demanded.

James closed his eyes and took a shallow breath, then he turned the handle and opened the door. Meredith couldn't watch and turned her head and looked the other way. The soft sounds of sniffling came from his mother. Mr. Merritt dropped his head, and his hand went to his forehead, rubbing his furrowed brows. Jamey's eyes followed him as he left the car door ajar and moved toward the back of the car. James used the trunk for support as he walked, and when he reached the other side of the car, he opened Meredith's door.

He braced himself against the car, his ribs raging with pain, and he knelt down in front of Meredith. He couldn't look her in the eyes, so he looked at her hand instead and at the fake band around her finger.

"I want to try to be your husband, and I want to try to be his father." He grabbed her hand and drew it to his face. He rested his forehead in her palm. Her fingers stroked his hair. *This feels good*, he thought. *This feels really good.* He kissed her hand and braced himself to stand.

"I'm tired of being haunted by shadows. I'm tired of running and I'm tired of hiding. I should have died on that train, but instead it chewed me up and spit me out."

Meredith searched his eyes for sincerity.

"I know you don't believe me. I've never given you reason to. And this won't be easy for either of us. I know I have a lot to learn." He pulled her closer to smell her chamomile hair.

Meredith took a deep breath, relieved and thankful that this was happening. "Where do we start?" Meredith asked. "I don't know where to start."

"I have some money saved. First we'll buy a house near my parents, as long as that's okay with you," he said to his parents. His mother smiled through her tears; his father put his hand on his wife's shoulder and squeezed.

"I'm sure to be deployed again, and then Mom and Dad will be close to help you with Jamey. And I would like to personally deliver your current house keys back into the hands of your father."

"That's probably not the best idea," Meredith said. "He's not a big fan of yours."

"If he wants to punch me, he can punch me. But I've a mind to punch him right back for disowning his daughter. Then again," he considered, "maybe he regrets some of the decisions he's made too.

"Then we'll find a preacher and we'll get married. And I promise, you'll have a real ring." He kissed her knuckles and her fake wedding band. "And, Meredith, I'm really so sorry."

Edwards was right, James thought as he pulled Meredith close to him. *Men should be allowed to cry.* He let the tears fall and tried not to be embarrassed by it, then reached down to Meredith's hand and spun the band on her finger.

Luther was right, too, and he heard the words echoed again, *Forgiveness, boys, is a beautiful thing.*

Acknowledgments

My many thanks to those who assisted in this potentially daunting process:

To Truett Buie for several swift kicks in the rear.

To Karli Jackson for her patience and encouragement as my developmental editor.

To Erika S. Nein for her keen eyes as my copy editor.

To Melissa Long, Amy Ashby, Mindy Kuhn, and the Warren Publishing staff for their professionalism, design, and steadfast advocacy for this book.

To my husband, Ernie, for his eternal support and patience, especially while having to listen to long intervals of my verbal musings.

To my girls, Audrey and Abbey, for never questioning or bemoaning the countless hours spent in the loft.

To God for all things.

When daylight broke on the morning of December 16, 1943, authorities witnessed the grim reality of the total devastation caused by the wreck of the Tamiami Champion. A crane prepares to begin clearing the charred wreckage from the tracks in the rural community of Rennert, North Carolina.

CPSIA information can be obtained
at www.ICGtesting.com
Printed in the USA
BVHW041239230223
659088BV00004B/284/J